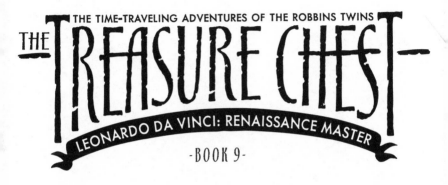

THE TIME-TRAVELING ADVENTURES OF THE ROBBINS TWINS

THE TREASURE CHEST

LEONARDO DA VINCI: RENAISSANCE MASTER

-BOOK 9-

BY *NEW YORK TIMES* BEST-SELLING AUTHOR

ANN HOOD

Grosset & Dunlap
An Imprint of Penguin Group (USA) LLC

For the Masciarottes

GROSSET & DUNLAP
Published by the Penguin Group
Penguin Group (USA) LLC, 375 Hudson Street, New York, New York 10014, USA

USA | Canada | UK | Ireland | Australia | New Zealand | India | South Africa | China

penguin.com
A Penguin Random House Company

Text copyright © 2014 by Ann Hood. Art copyright © 2014 by Denis Zilber. All rights reserved. Published by Grosset & Dunlap,
a division of Penguin Young Readers Group, 345 Hudson Street, New York, New York 10014.
GROSSET & DUNLAP is a trademark of Penguin Group (USA) LLC.
Printed in the USA.

Library of Congress Cataloging-in-Publication Data is available.

Design by Giuseppe Castellano.
Map illustration by Giuseppe Castellano and © 2013 by Penguin Group (USA) LLC.

ISBN 978-0-448-46769-6 (pbk)   10 9 8 7 6 5 4 3 2 1
ISBN 978-0-448-46768-9 (hc)   10 9 8 7 6 5 4 3 2 1

CHAPTER 1

THE MISSING EGG

Standing in The Treasure Chest as the late-afternoon sun sent rays of colored light through the stained-glass window and across the parquet floor, Felix thought the room looked sad. All of the items seemed ordinary somehow. Maybe it had to do with that late-afternoon light, which was dim and fading. Felix had never noticed the fraying around the edges of the carpet from Ashgabat in Turkmenistan where, according to Great-Uncle Thorne, the most beautiful carpets were made. The desk and shelves, their wood probably once gleaming, looked dull. Or maybe it was the items themselves, the gold nugget and test tubes and all the things filling the room, dusty and neglected.

Felix tried to imagine Phinneas Pickworth filling

this room, coming back to Elm Medona from Turkmenistan or Persia or the Amazon with his precious items. How excited he must have been to unpack his trunk and remove the carefully wrapped treasures! Felix narrowed his eyes, as if he could almost see his great-great-grandfather here, lifting an object close to his eyes to examine it. He would have smiled as he did. Satisfied. Delighted. Eager.

"Have you heard a word I've said?" Great-Uncle Thorne's voice boomed.

Felix stared a moment longer at the spot where a trick of light beneath the stained-glass window seemed to reveal a vague figure.

Felix blinked.

No, he convinced himself, it was just a shadow cast from the high shelf against that wall.

A cold breeze blew through The Treasure Chest, rifling the papers on the desk and sending goose bumps up Felix's arm.

Whatever was beneath the window—ghost or shadow—vanished. But near where it had appeared, something glistened gold. Felix felt that the object was beckoning him. Rubbing his arms to warm himself, he walked toward it.

But Great-Uncle Thorne reached out a gnarled and liver-spotted hand to stop him.

"Does the fact that the Ziff twins are missing have no impact on you at all?" he shouted, lowering his face to Felix's eye level.

"It does," Felix said, looking past Great-Uncle Thorne's voluminous white eyebrows to the twinkling object across the room.

"It, uh, impacts me," he managed.

And it did. Of course.

Maisie and Felix had left the Ziff twins in the Congo facing all sorts of danger: wild beasts, poisonous snakes, tropical diseases. While they had lived in homey comfort with Amelia Earhart in Iowa, fishing and riding rides at the state fair, the Ziff twins had been dodging calamity. At least Felix *hoped* they'd dodged calamity. He couldn't let himself think the worst. And now Great-Uncle Thorne had insisted they accompany him here to The Treasure Chest, even though their father was downstairs, no longer engaged to Agatha the Great, sitting with their surprised mother.

But despite all of that, Felix could not stop staring at the object, which as he slipped out of Great-Uncle

Thorne's grip and inched toward it, appeared to be a highly decorated egg.

"What in tarnation are you staring at?" Great-Uncle Thorne said so loudly that the globe on a shelf vibrated.

"That," Felix said, pointing.

Maisie, who had been quietly listening to Great-Uncle Thorne's hypotheses about what might have happened to the Ziff twins, stepped forward and followed Felix's pointing finger with her eyes.

"What?" she asked, unimpressed.

"Honestly, boy," Great-Uncle Thorne said, shaking his head, "your friends . . . No! Your cousins! . . . are missing, and you suddenly become mesmerized by a gaggle of objects."

"Not a gaggle of objects," Felix said. "Just the egg. The one that's . . ." He struggled for the right word. *Twinkling* sounded too light, *glowing* too strong. "Shining," he said finally, though that wasn't quite right, either.

"A shining egg?" Maisie repeated.

Great-Uncle Thorne tapped his walking stick on the floor three times, loud. It happened to be the walking stick Maisie liked least, with a crystal globe at the top, each continent etched in miniature on it, and along the length of the ivory stick itself the name of every country in the world had been carved. There were so many countries that their names carved there like that gave the impression of an intricate design. But up close you could make out the words— many of them, like Rhodesia, no longer even countries. *I think it's cool*, Felix had said when Maisie told him the walking stick gave her the creeps. *Countries that don't even exist anymore?* she'd said with a shudder. *And a stick made out of some poor elephant's tusk?*

"Actually," Great-Uncle Thorne said when he saw her staring at it now, "this walking stick was made by a witch doctor in Uganda for my father."

"It's illegal to kill elephants for their tusks, you know," Maisie told him.

"Elephant?" he said, his eyes blazing. "My dear child, this is made from the tusk of the rare white rhinoceros!"

"Even worse," Maisie said, her eyes blazing right back at Great-Uncle Thorne. "White rhinoceroses are an endangered species!"

"That egg," Felix said softly.

Both Maisie and Great-Uncle Thorne watched him as he gently lifted the egg from its place among the fossils and feathers.

The small bells from the yoke of a yak tinkled as another cold breeze blew through The Treasure Chest.

The egg was the most magnificent thing Felix had ever seen.

Heavy in his hand, larger than a baseball, beneath its ornamentation the egg was the purest white. Whiter than fresh snow. Whiter than clouds or angel hair. Four ribbons of gold radiated from its top, along the delicate curve of the egg, all the way to the bottom. Each ribbon had a different motif carved into it. Cherubs. Roses. Wolves' heads. And what appeared to be interlocking letter *R*s.

Then there were the jewels. Sapphires and diamonds bigger than marbles formed a cap at the top and covered the bottom. They sparkled as if they had just been polished, revealing every shade of blue imaginable. Cobalt and navy and midnight and sky. The diamonds, too, were different shades. Champagne and pink and yellow and eggshell.

Felix stroked the top of the egg, marveling at how many diamonds and sapphires covered it. All of them a slightly different color, all of them so smooth.

Except one.

His hand paused over a particularly deep-blue sapphire. So dark, in fact, that it almost looked black. This sapphire did not shine like the others. It was dull and rougher cut.

"Put! That! Down!" Great-Uncle Thorne ordered.

When Felix didn't obey fast enough, Great-Uncle Thorne poked him in the knees with his walking stick.

"Ouch!" Felix exclaimed, holding on even tighter to the egg.

"Give it to me this instant," Great-Uncle Thorne demanded.

He didn't wait for Felix to hand over the egg. He just grabbed it from him.

"Hey!" Felix protested.

But Great-Uncle Thorne was not listening. His eyes took in every inch of the egg. His hands ran over its surface slowly, as if they were memorizing it.

Not memorizing, Felix realized as he watched Great-Uncle Thorne. The opposite. *Remembering* it.

"Have you been here the whole time?" Great-Uncle Thorne whispered in a raspy voice to the egg.

Tears sprang to his eyes and fell down his cheeks.

"What in the world is going on?" Maisie asked, confused.

Was she the only one worrying about Hadley and Rayne? Was she the only one who didn't care an ounce about this fancy egg?

Felix put his hand on Maisie's shoulder.

"It's the missing egg," he said, tears in his eyes, too.

"What missing egg?" Maisie asked.

Great-Uncle Thorne managed to lift his eyes away from the egg and look at Felix and Maisie.

"All those years she accused me of stealing it," he said. "And it was here the whole time."

"Who?" Maisie asked.

"Great-Aunt Maisie," Felix said softly, for Great-Uncle Thorne's attention had gone back to the egg. He was tracing the design on each gold ribbon and whispering to himself as he did.

"Don't you remember?" Felix said to Maisie. "She had her Fabergé egg, and you broke the code to open it. But she told us that Thorne had stolen another one. That's why they never spoke again."

Great-Uncle Thorne turned to face them. In that one instant, Felix thought, he looked like the very, very old man that he was.

"That's one reason," Great-Uncle Thorne said. "But also because I kept her from staying with Harry."

He added, "Harry Houdini."

Maisie and Felix nodded.

"But I knew what it would mean if she stayed. And I didn't want to lose her," Great-Uncle Thorne said.

Although he was speaking to them, he had a faraway look in his eyes.

"When we got back, she was furious," he continued, "and she threatened to lock The Treasure Chest and throw away the key. *You've kept me from my one true love, Thorne*, she told me. *And I'll never forgive you for that.*"

Great-Uncle Thorne's gaze settled on Maisie and Felix.

"You didn't know her the way I did. She was strong willed and stubborn and thickheaded. And," he said with a sigh, "utterly marvelous."

Felix tried to reconcile the old Great-Aunt Maisie that he'd known with the girl Great-Uncle Thorne described. He thought of the picture on the wall of the Grand Staircase, and the glimpse of her as that girl when they had met Harry Houdini. But still, to him, Great-Aunt Maisie was a crabby, snobbish old woman.

"And then," Great-Uncle Thorne said with a sigh, "we discovered that the egg was missing. How she carried on! Accusing me of thievery. And worse. The more I insisted I had nothing to do with its disappearance, the more she insisted I did. There were no more trips to The Treasure Chest. No more midnight swims or Newport parties or adventures. That autumn I went to school in England and I never spoke to or saw my sister again. Until I came back last winter. And then . . ."

Great-Uncle Thorne dropped his head in his hands and began to sob.

"There, there," Felix said, rubbing Great-Uncle Thorne's back the way his own mother did when Felix was upset.

"But . . . ," Maisie began.

Then she waited, because with Great-Uncle Thorne sobbing like this, it probably wasn't the time to ask.

Great-Uncle Thorne raised his tearstained face. "What?" he asked her.

"Well, Great-Aunt Maisie had her egg. We saw it," Maisie said, looking to Felix, who nodded in confirmation.

"And I presume you have yours?" Maisie asked rhetorically. "So this one is the egg Phinneas Pickworth gave to Ariane when you and Great-Aunt Maisie were born?"

"The very one," Great-Uncle Thorne said, and sobbed even harder. He held the egg close now, like a long-lost friend.

Maisie waited until Great-Uncle Thorne's sobs quieted.

"But what's so special about this egg? I mean," she added quickly, "other than the fact that it was your mother's and everyone thought it was missing."

Great-Uncle Thorne took a deep breath.

Maisie and Felix held their breath.

"I don't know," Great-Uncle Thorne said.

"What do you mean, you don't know?" Maisie, puzzled, asked him.

Great-Uncle Thorne held the egg at arm's length and studied it. Maisie and Felix studied it, too.

The Treasure Chest grew very quiet.

"Yes," he said finally. "It is special because it

belonged to our mother, a woman we, sadly, never knew."

He paused again, took another deep breath, then continued.

"And of course, the fact that it was missing— stolen, we all believed—makes finding it even more wonderful."

"So maybe that's it?" Felix said. "Those facts alone make it a very special egg. And make it even more exciting that we found it again after all this time."

But Great-Uncle Thorne shook his head.

"You see," he said, one finger rubbing the odd sapphire, "unlike my Fabergé egg or Maisie's, this one has never been opened."

"Why not?" Maisie asked.

"Inside is the key," Great-Uncle Thorne said.

"The key to . . . ?" Maisie prodded.

"My mother was French," Great-Uncle Thorne said. "You know that, *oui*?"

"Is that why everyone here speaks French and eats French food?" Felix said, thinking of the *moules frites* and *duck à l'orange* and *pot-au-feu* that showed up for dinner almost every night.

"And you know that *Elm Medona* is an anagram for—"

"*Lame demon*," Maisie interrupted, frustrated.

"Which comes from the French novel *Paris Before Man*, which was written by Pierre Boitard in 1861 and which is about time travel," Great-Uncle Thorne said.

"What does any of this have to do with the egg?" Maisie said in exasperation.

"The key is in this egg," Great-Uncle Thorne said.

Maisie opened her mouth to ask, again, *What key?*

But Great-Uncle Thorne held up his hand to stop her.

"I have no idea what the key opens. Or what it means," he said. "I only know that my father, Phinneas Pickworth," he added, as if Maisie and Felix might have forgotten who his father was, "ordered Maisie and me to never, under any circumstances, take out the key unless he told us it was time."

"That's why it was so terrible when it went missing," Maisie said, thinking out loud.

"I know that if we lift this sapphire, something

will open," Great-Uncle Thorne said, his long fingers resting on the dark sapphire.

"I know that whatever opens will reveal another door, and that door requires a code to open it," he said. "But whatever the implications of all of that are . . . well . . ."

Great-Uncle Thorne shrugged.

"For now," he said, "I will take this to my room with me and reunite it with the other two."

He began to walk toward the door.

"Wait!" Maisie called to him. "What about Hadley and Rayne?"

Great-Uncle Thorne, baffled, looked at her.

"The Ziff twins?" she reminded him.

"Ah! Yes. Very troublesome."

He considered for a moment then said, "I'll return this to my room and then come back here to discuss the Ziff twins."

Felix watched Great-Uncle Thorne leave The Treasure Chest.

"Weird, right?" Maisie said. "The mysterious key. The right time . . ."

"Mmmm," Felix said, because that was all he could think to say.

What he knew, what he felt certain of, was that the egg had not been in The Treasure Chest all these years after all. Someone, or something, had returned it today, this very afternoon. And Felix had a terrible feeling that whatever that key opened, the time had come to use it.

CHAPTER 2

THE RETURN OF THE ZIFF TWINS

M inutes passed.

Then more minutes passed.

Maisie sighed. "That's it," she said. "I'm going back downstairs. I can't waste another minute waiting for Great-Uncle Thorne to come back while Dad is downstairs maybe convincing Mom to marry him again."

She delivered this while she walked across The Treasure Chest to the door. Suddenly, to Maisie, a whole world of possibility lay not in time travel here in this room like it used to, but downstairs with her parents. Maybe they were already making plans. Maybe they were in one of those kisses they used to do sometimes, when her father dipped her mother backward over his arm and bent over to kiss her. Maybe this entire year was like a bad dream of broken homes and broken hearts, a dream that was about to end.

Maisie stood in the doorway, bouncing up and down on her toes, ready to go.

"Coming?" she asked Felix.

Felix hesitated. "What about the Ziffs?" he asked, glancing around as if the the twins might be lurking behind a shelf, or about to drop in from the Congo all of a sudden.

"Great-Uncle Thorne can figure that out," she said, only a little guiltily. "I mean, Mom and Dad are together downstairs. And there's no Agatha—"

"Well, there is a Bruce Fishbaum," Felix reminded her.

"How in the world could anyone choose Bruce Fishbaum over Dad?" Maisie shrieked.

Now Felix sighed. If he could explain the confusing way the human heart worked, he would. But he had no idea.

"Bruce Fishbaum has nautically themed clothes!" Maisie said. "He wears purple! A lot!"

Felix shrugged. "I just think—"

"I don't care what you think," Maisie said. "I'm going downstairs, where I'll maybe even celebrate their reunion."

With that, she left, making sure to stomp out so that Felix was absolutely sure she was fed up with him.

From the top of the stairs, Maisie heard the most beautiful sound she could imagine: the sound of her parents laughing together. She paused to take it in, her father's husky chuckle and her mother's tinkling-bell laugh, the one that she perfected doing summer-stock musicals.

Maisie breathed in the laughter and then ran down the stairs, following the sound through the Library and into the Cigar Room, which was little used now but once was where Phinneas Pickworth and his cronies would meet after dinner for cognac and cigars, retelling their great adventures.

The Cigar Room had striped wallpaper and a zebra-skin rug; the furniture was all heavy and ornate and made of teak by a craftsman in Indonesia. Despite all the time that had passed since Phinneas Pickworth was in the room, the smell of cigar smoke still lingered.

Maisie's father sat perched on the corner of the long narrow table that held crystal decanters of cognacs and single-malt whiskeys, some of them still holding the amber liquids. Her mother looked up at him from the largest, most ornate chair, the one that looked like a throne. And she was smiling, a big toothy smile. When Maisie cleared her throat, neither of them even turned toward her.

"Hello?" Maisie said.

"Oh!" her mother said, color rushing to her cheeks. "Maisie."

"That's the one," Maisie said. "What are you two up to?"

"Your father is just . . ." Her mother frowned. "He's just making me laugh, that's all."

"The foibles of love," her father said.

Maisie took this as hopeful.

"Wait until Mom tells you about Bruce Fishbaum," she said wickedly. "He wears purple."

"Maisie!" her mother said.

"He does," Maisie insisted. "Also, his ties all have a nautical theme."

Her father stifled a smile.

"Jake," her mother said, getting up stiffly, "you

were just about to leave, weren't you?"

"I was," he said, hopping down from the table. "But I'll be at the Viking for a few days so I can see you two," he said, pointing at Maisie.

The smell of dog overtook the faint aroma of cigars as James Ferocious wandered into the Cigar Room.

"Ugh!" Maisie's mother groaned. "What are we going to do with this monstrosity?"

"Tell you what," her father said, "I'll come by first thing and take him to the vet and to a groomer for a bath."

"Deal," her mother said.

As she walked out past James Ferocious, she wrinkled her nose.

"How old is this dog?" she said. "He smells ancient."

"Only a hundred years old," Maisie said.

"Very funny, Maisie," her mother said, shaking her head.

Upstairs in The Treasure Chest, Felix waited for Great-Uncle Thorne to return. He couldn't help but start to worry—about the Ziff twins and the Fabergé egg that had mysteriously reappeared and about Maisie. One thing Felix felt fairly certain about was that their parents were not going to get married again. At least not to each other. But he could see that Maisie was already imagining it, already planning on all of them being a family again.

Felix picked up a magnifying glass and peered through it, enjoying how everything on the desk came into focus. The delicate marks on the quill pen on the desk. The smudges on a test tube. He rummaged through the objects, keeping the magnifying glass pressed against his eye.

A small gold cylinder rolled out from beneath a dried corsage. Felix lowered the magnifying glass and picked up the cylinder. It was heavy but unremarkable. Except for the odd symbol on one end. Felix frowned, trying to determine what that symbol was. A coat of arms, maybe? The center almost looked like the design on one of his father's ties, but there were definitely flowers on it, too. And a thin layer of dark red covered it. Paint? Or . . . Felix shivered . . . blood?

Great-Uncle Thorne's noisy return right then made Felix jump.

"What's that you're examining?" Great-Uncle Thorne demanded.

Felix held it up, squinting.

"Hmmm," Great-Uncle Thorne said. "It's a seal. You melt wax onto the back of an envelope and then press that into it. Leaves the mark of . . ."

He leaned closer to see what was on the end.

"Ah! That's the *giglio*. The emblem of Florence."

"What's a *giglio*?" Felix asked him.

"I'm sure even you've seen the fleur-de-lis on flags and coats of arms?"

"Fleur . . . what?"

"Philistines! You and that surly sister of yours!"

Felix studied the symbol again. "Maybe I've seen something like it somewhere," he said.

"Somewhere?" Great-Uncle Thorne repeated, raising his arms and his eyes upward as if praying for help. "The fleur-de-lis has been the enduring symbol of France for centuries!"

"Maybe that's where—"

"And the arms of the king of Spain!"

"Oh, maybe that's where—"

"And the grand duke of Luxembourg!"

"Well, then, gee, sure," Felix said.

"But *that* is the *giglio*, which distinguishes itself by showing a blossom, always red, comprised of three main petals and three thin stamens arranged symmetrically."

Felix smiled, relieved. If this seal was pressed into red wax, then that's what he saw. Not blood, but the remnants of wax.

"In fact," Great-Uncle Thorne was saying, "the floral symbol goes back to ancient times, to 59 BC, when Florence was founded around the time of the Roman celebration of spring and the white iris florentina was in full bloom. Why, the Romans even called the city Florentia, and held festivities there to honor the goddess Flora. If you're ever lucky enough to visit Florence, you'll see the *giglio* everywhere. On the Ponte Vecchio and the Duomo—"

"I thought you said the gi . . . gig . . ."

"*Giglio!*" Great-Uncle Thorne boomed in exasperation.

"Right," Felix said. "I thought you said it was red."

"And?"

"Well, you said the iris florentina was *white*."

To Felix's surprise, Great-Uncle Thorne grinned at him. "You're right! Good observation! The colors were inverted in 1266. The Guelphs took control of Florence and used a red lily on a white background on their flags. And so it has remained ever since."

Great-Uncle Thorne got that faraway look that often crossed over him.

And Felix took that opportunity to put the seal in his pocket. He would write Lily Goldberg a letter, he decided, and melt red wax onto the back of the envelope, and press the *giglio* into it. He could picture her all the way in Cleveland puzzling over the symbol. When she Googled it, she'd see that it was a lily! What a perfect plan, Felix decided.

But his delight faded when his very next thought was the Ziff twins' disappearance.

"Uncle Thorne?" Felix said softly.

Great-Uncle Thorne blinked several times, as if he were blinking away a memory.

"What about Rayne and Hadley?"

"Who?"

"The Ziff twins," Felix reminded him.

"Very troubling," Great-Uncle Thorne said. "Bothersome. Potentially catastrophic."

"Catastrophic?" Felix repeated with a quiver in his voice. He thought about how Hadley's curly black hair got even curlier in the damp Newport sea air, and how a glimpse of Rayne's hot-pink braces always made him smile, and how the Ziff twins were the only friends he and Maisie actually shared, and the next thing he knew, Felix burst into tears.

Great-Uncle Thorne looked at Felix, horrified.

"Now, now," he said awkwardly. "We'll figure out how to get them back."

"But how can we possibly?" Felix blurted, which made him cry harder.

"We'll . . . why . . . You and Maisie can go back to the Congo and *get* them!" Great-Uncle Thorne banged his walking stick for emphasis, and grinned triumphantly.

But the last thing Felix wanted to do was go back to the Congo. And besides, Hadley and Rayne had the object.

"This is hopeless," Felix groaned.

"Nothing is hopeless," Great-Uncle Thorne said unconvincingly.

Felix's crying slowed. He hiccupped and wiped the tears off his face.

"*This* is," he said.

But as soon as he said it, Felix felt the slightest

hint of a cool breeze. He could tell Great-Uncle Thorne felt it, too, by the way his eyebrows lifted and his nose twitched.

Felix smelled a hint of something sweet, and heard a faint sound from somewhere far, far away.

And then—just like that!—Hadley and Rayne dropped into The Treasure Chest.

Except for his father showing up at Elm Medona this afternoon, Felix had never been so happy to see someone.

"You're alive!" he shouted as he ran over to them and spontaneously pulled them both into a hug.

"No thanks to you," Rayne said, wriggling away from him.

"We were going to get eaten by lions," Felix tried to explain.

But Rayne held up her hand to stop him. "Don't bother," she said. "You have no idea what we've been through. Lions. Hah!"

"Curious," Great-Uncle Thorne said thoughtfully. "Since we've never had travelers left behind, I can't explain what's happened here or why. But hallelujah! You're back!"

Felix turned to Hadley, who was still standing in

a half-hug with him. Her hair looked like corkscrew pasta standing up all around her head.

"I'm sorry," he said to her. "First Maisie got kidnapped by a silverback gorilla, and then I practically got bitten by a huge poisonous snake, and then—"

"The lions," Hadley finished for him. "I know. I saw you."

"You were *there*?"

Hadley nodded. "I was on the other side of that pride—"

"—and I was being held hostage by natives!" Rayne said indignantly. "They had never seen hair like mine before and they wanted it. All of it." She smoothed her hair nervously as she talked. "The whole village came to stare at me and touch my hair, and then the chief started making preparations to cut it all off—"

"And then you escaped," Hadley reminded her.

"Barely," Rayne muttered.

"Meanwhile," Hadley said, "I saw those lions, and I saw you and Maisie, but I was afraid to call out to you. I mean, I didn't want the lions to see me. And then in a flash you two completely vanished." She snapped her fingers. "Faster than that!"

"We ended up in St. Louis," Felix said.

"Missouri?" Rayne asked, incredulous.

Felix nodded. "And then we went to Kansas, and you'll never guess who we met."

When neither Ziff twin tried to guess, he said, "Amelia Earhart!"

"Well," Rayne huffed, "while you were in *Kansas* with Amelia Earhart, I had to spend the night alone in the jungle with a tribe chasing me, and Hadley lost."

Felix cringed at the thought. The jungle had been scary enough in the daytime. He couldn't imagine what it was like at night.

As if she'd read his mind, Rayne continued. "Civets," she said, "are nocturnal. They are creepy little animals that come out around midnight to hunt. Also badgers and other animals I can't even describe. And of course, leopards."

"But you were fine," Hadley said.

"Until the elephants," Rayne said.

"Well, the elephants were kind of scary," Hadley agreed.

"Kind of? They *charged* us! A whole herd of them!"

"But we managed to escape," Hadley said proudly.

"You got charged by a herd of elephants?" Felix sputtered. "And then what?"

Hadley smiled at Felix.

"And then," she said, "we found Amy Pickworth."

CHAPTER 3

911

Even though Maisie did not like that her father left, she took comfort in the fact that James Ferocious stayed by her side and followed her up the Grand Staircase, and along the hallway that led to the wall with the special place to press. When the wall magically opened, James Ferocious yelped. Maisie liked that, too. She bent and petted him behind his ears until he closed his eyes in sheer happiness.

"Come on, boy," she whispered.

James Ferocious groaned a little and pushed his big smelly head against her leg for more petting.

"We've got things to do," Maisie told the dog. But she still had to tug on his collar to get him to come with her.

The staircase looked small beneath the big dog, who galumphed up it awkwardly, his claws scratching as he kept his balance. James Ferocious was the first one to reach The Treasure Chest, but instead of going inside, he slid to a halt at the door and let out a mournful howl.

Maisie came up right behind him.

She stopped dead in her tracks, too. Though instead of a howl, she gasped.

"Oh no!"

Three pairs of eyes turned toward her.

"Is he . . . ?" Maisie began, unable to say the actual word.

Great-Uncle Thorne was splayed on the floor of The Treasure Chest, his face a ghostly white, his eyes closed, and a thin line of drool coming from his gaping mouth.

Hadley kneeled beside him, her ear pressed to his chest.

From here, Great-Uncle Thorne looked oddly small and very, very old.

"His heart's beating!" Hadley announced, and it seemed to Maisie that everyone and everything gave an enormous sigh of relief. Even James Ferocious.

Even The Treasure Chest itself.

"Face pale, raise the tail," Rayne instructed. She'd been a Girl Scout for exactly two weeks, long enough to earn exactly one merit badge. Luckily it was in first aid.

Felix grabbed a needlepoint pillow from a small footstool. Like everything in The Treasure Chest, that pillow was old. The fabric had faded from white to gray, and the crooked stitching on it was fraying. As Felix slid it beneath Great-Uncle Thorne's head, he noted the date stitched there: 1776.

"Raise the *tail*," Rayne said.

When Felix looked confused, she said, "His *feet*."

Why she would call feet a tail, Felix didn't know, but he obeyed.

Great-Uncle Thorne's feet seemed to weigh a ton, two heavy deadweights in what he called his house slippers, black velvet things with three interlocked gold *P*s on the tops.

James Ferocious refused to enter The Treasure Chest, but Maisie cautiously walked in. Great-Uncle Thorne might have a heartbeat, but he looked about as awful as a person could look.

Rayne, all serious, stuck two of her fingers beneath

Great-Uncle Thorne's nose.

"He's breathing, all right," she said. "I think the old bugger just fainted, that's all."

"Shouldn't we *do* something?" Felix asked, not convinced that this wasn't an emergency. "Get smelling salts or call nine-one-one or something?"

Everyone turned to Rayne for her opinion. She considered, then said, "Cold compresses."

"Could you speak English, please?" Felix grumbled.

"Cold damp facecloths," she said, sighing.

Felix jumped to his feet and ran out to get them, muttering, "Cold *compresses*," as he did.

It wasn't until Felix was gone and Maisie stood alone with the prone Great-Uncle Thorne and the Ziff twins that she realized that they—the Ziff twins—were back. And seemingly alive and well.

"Hadley!" she shrieked, and hugged her friend. "Rayne!"

Rayne shook her head. "No hugging during first aid," she said.

"You're both okay," Maisie said, another rush of relief washing over her.

"No thanks to you," Rayne said.

Maisie looked at her, surprised. "We were about to be eaten by lions!" she began.

But Rayne shook her head again. "Lions? I was kidnapped and almost scalped, chased by a herd of elephants—"

"Saved by the cold compresses," Hadley said as Felix rushed back in with two jewel-toned, monogrammed facecloths dripping cold water.

"On the forehead," Rayne ordered.

Felix slapped one on Great-Uncle Thorne's furrowed forehead, causing the old man to practically leap to his feet.

"What in tarnation?" he shouted.

As soon as he sat up, however, he had to lie right back down.

"Dizzy," he said.

"Stay put," Rayne told him. "You fainted," she added.

"I've never fainted in my life," Great-Uncle Thorne protested weakly.

Water dripped down his face, making him look even more pathetic. But at least his cheeks now had two hot pink spots, one on each, which looked even pinker against the ghastly white.

"Well," Hadley said, "there's a first time for everything, then. Because you fainted as soon as I said—"

Rayne shushed her sister.

"Let the man recover," she said.

Then she turned to Felix. "FYI, damp does not mean dripping wet."

"What did you say?" Maisie asked Hadley.

Hadley leaned in close to Maisie and whispered, "We found her."

"Her who?"

"Amy Pickworth."

And even though they were whispering, Great-Uncle Thorne's eyes grew wide and his face lost the pink spots. He lifted his head as if to speak, but instead, once again, his eyes rolled back in his head, and his head dropped with a thud to the floor. Just like that, he fainted for the second time in his life.

With two soggy facecloths on his forehead, Great-Uncle Thorne's eyelids fluttered open.

"Where?" he asked. "What?"

Then his eyes closed again, and this time a strange release of air escaped from his lungs, like the bellows he used to stoke the fire in the Library fireplace.

From the doorway, James Ferocious began to bark and pace back and forth.

Hadley put her ear to Great-Uncle Thorne's chest, and Rayne placed her fingers beneath his nose.

A clock somewhere in The Treasure Chest ticked noisily and then grew quiet.

"His heart," Hadley said without lifting her head. "It's . . . muffled."

"I'm not sure he's breathing," Rayne said. "It might be time to start CPR."

This last she said with a voice so panicked that James Ferocious barked louder and paced more frantically.

Felix took stock of what he was seeing: Maisie's mouth opened in fear; Hadley's ear pressed against what Great-Uncle Thorne called his dressing gown, a ridiculous moss-green silk thing; Rayne desperately searching for a puff of air from his nostrils; James Ferocious barking and pacing; and Great-Uncle Thorne as white as marble.

That was enough for Felix.

He ran out of The Treasure Chest, down the stairway, down the long carpeted hallway, past the tapestries from the Middle Ages, down the Grand

Staircase, past the photo of Great-Aunt Maisie as a young girl with Great-Uncle Thorne poking his head into the picture, slipping and sliding across the shiny polished floor of the foyer, and into the Library, where the ridiculous old-fashioned phone sat.

With trembling fingers, Felix put his finger first into the nine on the dial, and swept it slowly all the way across and back. Then, into the one, which at least was faster, and then swept the one again.

He waited what seemed like forever, but really was no time at all, until a nasally female voice said, "Nine-one-one."

Felix shouted into the heavy receiver.

He shouted the address of Elm Medona.

He shouted, "I think my great-uncle has had a heart attack or something."

He shouted, "Come fast!"

From the Cigar Room his mother called, "What's all the shouting?"

The 911 lady said, "Calm down, son. You're doing fine. An ambulance is on its way. Stay on the line until they get there."

Felix could not calm down.

He kept repeating the address.

"Elm Medona," he shouted into the heavy receiver. "Maybe you know it?"

"I do," the 911 lady said.

"What's all the shouting, Felix?" his mother called again.

Now he heard her coming toward the Library, and way off in the distance, a siren.

"I hear it," he told the 911 lady. "The ambulance."

"Stay on the line, son," she said. "You're doing fine."

The sound of the siren grew closer.

His mother appeared in the doorway, irritated.

"Enough surprises," she said. "A dog. Your father. I'm trying to get some work done."

"It's here, I think," Felix shouted to the 911 lady.

The 911 lady said, "Go open the door, son. Let them in."

Felix dropped the receiver and pushed past his mother.

"Hey!" his mother said.

But Felix didn't pause.

By now, Great-Uncle Thorne could be dead.

Don't cry, he told himself. He had too much to do.

Even from all the way down here, he could hear

James Ferocious barking incessantly. Felix thought about how dogs—or maybe cats?—could predict earthquakes and deaths in hospitals and all sorts of catastrophes. The word *catastrophe* almost made him cry again, since, like, an hour ago Great-Uncle Thorne had used it.

But now Felix was at the door, and now he was opening it, and now four men with a stretcher and all kinds of medical equipment were storming into the Grand Foyer.

"Where is he?" one of them asked.

Without answering, Felix began the reverse run up the Grand Staircase, past the photo of young Maisie and Thorne, past the Middle Ages tapestries, down the corridor to the spot where the wall gaped open, up the stairway, past a barking James Ferocious, and into The Treasure Chest.

"I can't hear his heartbeat," Hadley said through her tears.

"Sir," Rayne said, standing as soon as she saw the first EMT, "I did the ABC's of CPR."

Her voice quivered. "Airway. Breathing—"

"Out of the way, sweetheart," the EMT said.

The other three EMTs pushed quickly through

the door of The Treasure Chest.

One of them knocked into the desk with the big machine he was carrying.

Phinneas Pickworth's treasures that were there flew to the floor.

Something shattered.

"Pulse!" an EMT shouted, and then said a bunch of numbers.

"Oxygen!" another one shouted. More numbers.

Great-Uncle Thorne looked worse than before. Not only was his face as white as marble, it seemed like marble—cold and stony and still.

"Get these kids out of here," an EMT shouted.

Felix, Hadley, and Rayne skittered out, lingering with James Ferocious in the doorway.

Only Maisie couldn't move. She could only stare as they clapped something onto Great-Uncle Thorne's arm and something else onto his finger.

"Get that dog out of here," the same EMT shouted.

Felix grabbed James Ferocious's collar and tried to pull him away, but the dog wouldn't budge. Or stop barking.

"On my three," an EMT said.

The children watched as the EMTs rolled Great-

Uncle Thorne onto the stretcher, then lifted the stretcher high.

"What is going on?" Maisie and Felix's mother said, out of breath.

"Out of our way, ma'am," the EMTs ordered.

Everyone stepped aside as they carried Great-Uncle Thorne out of The Treasure Chest.

"Uncle Thorne," their mother cried.

She looked from Great-Uncle Thorne to the EMT vanishing down the staircase to the children and the dog huddled in the doorway of The Treasure Chest.

"What is going on?" she said again, but softly, as if she were asking herself.

"I have a merit badge in first aid," a tearful Rayne explained. "I even got a perfect score giving CPR to the Annie doll."

"He fainted," Hadley said, her voice full of wonder.

He *had* fainted, she told herself. The first time anyway, as soon as he heard her say that she met Amy Pickworth. So if Great-Uncle Thorne died, then it was all her fault. With this realization, Hadley, too, began to cry.

At the sight of his mother standing in the

doorway, Felix also burst into tears.

His mother patted Rayne on the back, touched Hadley's shoulder, and smoothed Felix's hair as she moved across the threshold and into The Treasure Chest, where Maisie sat sobbing on the floor in the same spot Great-Uncle Thorne had lain. Behind her, broken glass glittered like diamonds in the dying light.

"Mom," Maisie said, but that was all, because what was there to say?

Her mother looked at Maisie.

Then she looked up at the stained-glass window sending the day's last breath of light across the room. She looked at the window with the same expression she wore when she did a jigsaw puzzle. The expression seemed to say, *Ah! I see now how it all fits together.*

Her gaze drifted from the window to The Treasure Chest itself.

Like everybody who walks into The Treasure Chest for the first time, she could not take it all in. Her eyes flitted from test tubes to talismans to hunks of quartz and amethyst to the shelves groaning with objects; the cluttered desk; the tabletops obscured by stuff.

"What?" she began. But she couldn't articulate what she wanted to say.

She swallowed, took a breath, looked at Maisie. "What is this room?" she finally managed to ask. Maisie lifted her tearstained face to her mother. "The Treasure Chest," she said.

CHAPTER 4

RENAISSANCE MEANS REBIRTH

"Renaissance means rebirth," Miss Landers said. Except she wasn't saying it to Felix's class. She was saying it to the entire sixth grade. A special assembly had been called, and all of the sixth-graders were sitting in the auditorium where *The Crucible* would be performed in a few weeks.

"We are about to begin an exciting unit," Miss Landers continued. "It involves art, science . . ."

But Felix couldn't listen to what Miss Landers was saying.

Renaissance means rebirth.

Would Great-Uncle Thorne, lying in a coma at Newport General Hospital, be reborn?

Would his parents' marriage, despite Bruce

Fishbaum, finally be reborn?

Would Amy Pickworth, whose story still remained untold, be reborn?

How could he possibly listen to Miss Landers talk about something that happened centuries ago when right now his whole world needed to be reborn?

While Felix considered all of this, somehow the art teacher, Ms. Silva, had appeared at the microphone.

Ms. Silva wore long flowing caftans. Her hair, long and wavy, was streaked with gray. A large woman, she somehow managed to move gracefully, as if she were floating. Even when Felix, who did not take art, saw her in the hallways, she seemed to float in her colorful clothes, her multitude of bangle bracelets and bells around her ankles making a sound track to Ms. Silva.

"Oh, sixth-graders!" she crooned, clapping her hands together in front of the microphone and releasing more jingles and jangles than usual. "Oh, sixth-graders! The Renaissance! I will be your guide through Florence. I will show you art. And artists. And"—here she paused dramatically and took a breath so deep that the sound of it magnified through the microphone made everyone titter.

"And! Sixth-graders! You will learn the names of artists, like my personal favorite, Piero della Francesca. Artists so magnificent that . . ."

Ms. Silva became overcome by the magnificence of the Renaissance artists, and without finishing her talk, was led from the stage.

Miss Landers recovered quickly.

"Together, we will have a Renaissance fair, to which all of your parents will be invited. Jennifer Twill will play the *lira da braccio*, which is a Renaissance violin she has mastered."

The class snickered. Jennifer Twill did only odd things.

"Now, class, I want to remind you of Jennifer's hammered dulcimer performance at last year's Christmas party, and her wonderful contra dancing at the end-of-the-year talent show."

This only led to more snickering, but Miss Landers continued.

"*This* year, at the end of the unit, we will hold our own Renaissance fair. Ms. Silva will do workshops on masks, and Mrs. Witherspoon will hold cooking classes so that you can prepare a feast for the fair."

Miss Landers sighed happily.

"The Renaissance," she said.

Dear Lily,

A lot has been going on at Anne Hutchinson Elementary School. For one thing, there are new kids. Twins! For another thing, Maisie got the lead in the play, which is The Crucible. *(Maybe you are also reading this play? I like to think that sixth grades everywhere are doing the exact same thing, even in Cleveland.)*

And now we are beginning a unit on the Renaissance. We have to make masks with Ms. Silva and food with Mrs. Witherspoon and put on an entire fair. To tell you the truth, I kind of stopped listening during the assembly because so much is going on at Elm Medona. The biggest thing, the worst thing, is that Great-Uncle Thorne is in the intensive care unit of the hospital. My mother said it doesn't look good.

I know I have not been a good friend. I haven't stayed in touch the way I promised. Because I don't have an e-mail address, I couldn't e-mail you. But I could have written a real letter, like I'm doing now. Still, I think about you at least once every day. Sometimes even more.

Lily, Renaissance means rebirth. So now I am trying

to be reborn as a better friend.

Felix Robbins

PS Did you notice the red seal on the back of this envelope???????

PPS I hope you write back.

"Once," Jim Duncan said as he and Maisie and Felix walked to school the next day, "my family went to Florence. We spent three weeks in Italy. One in Rome. One in Venice. One in Florence."

"That's nice," Felix said, but he couldn't really listen. He could only think about the letter he mailed to Lily Goldberg in Cleveland last night. Part of him wished he hadn't mailed it. The other part wished she'd answer back as soon as she got it.

"Our father studied art in Florence when he was in college," Maisie said to Jim Duncan.

She wasn't really listening, either. She was thinking about how yesterday their father came to Elm Medona after they finished their homework and brought them out to the Thai place on Thames Street for dinner. She was thinking about how much she liked having her father so near.

Maybe Mom would like some Thai food, too? she'd

suggested as they walked down Memorial Boulevard.

She has to work late, he'd said, and Maisie couldn't figure out if he was sad about that or not.

And of course, underneath these thoughts, Maisie and Felix both couldn't stop thinking about Great-Uncle Thorne.

"I was only seven," Jim Duncan said. "But I remember some things. Like how hot it was in the Uffizi and how big the *David* is."

"Uh-huh," Felix said, to be polite. He knew the *David* was a sculpture by Michelangelo, because his father had a big book about Michelangelo with the *David* on the cover.

"The Uffizi's a huge museum," Jim Duncan said. He sighed. "It took practically forever to go through the thing."

Felix smiled, despite how heavy his heart felt. Jim Duncan had a way of telling him things without sounding like a know-it-all.

"Hey," Jim Duncan said, "I forgot to tell you. Guess who was in Newport this weekend?"

Felix shrugged.

"Lily Goldberg!" Jim Duncan said. "I saw her and her mother on Bowen's Wharf at the chowder place. I guess they had to finish up something about selling their house."

"What?" Felix said. "She was here?"

Jim Duncan immediately realized his mistake. "Well, maybe it wasn't her."

"Did you talk to her?"

"Well, maybe."

"I can't believe she was in Newport and didn't even tell me. I mean, us," Felix said, images of that letter crowding his brain. He thought about how carefully he'd written out her address, how he'd melted the red sealing wax on the back and pressed the seal into it.

Felix groaned. "I can't believe it," he said again.

Anne Hutchinson Elementary School appeared up ahead. Felix didn't think he could make it through the whole day at school. How could he listen to Ms. Silva and Miss Landers and everybody talking about the Renaissance while that stupid letter was on its way to Cleveland?

"I . . . I think I'm going to turn around," Felix said.

"What does that mean?" Maisie asked him.

"It means I think I'm going to go home. I think I'm sick."

"You can't just go home," Maisie said. "You at least have to go to the nurse and have her call Mom."

"I'll walk you to the nurse," Jim Duncan offered. By the look on his face, Felix could tell how awful he felt.

"No, it's okay. Thanks," Felix stammered. "I'm just going to go home."

Maisie and Jim looked at each other.

"Well . . . ," Jim said, because he didn't know what to say.

"Are you going to throw up or something?" Maisie asked.

"Yes," Felix lied, and clutched his stomach to be convincing.

"Then let us walk you to the nurse," Maisie insisted. "She'll take your temperature and let you lie down."

Of course that was the sensible thing to do. But Felix could not walk another step toward school. Without saying anything more, he turned around and began to run in the opposite direction. He wondered if that letter was already in some post office in Cleveland. Once, when he was in first grade, they'd gone on a field trip to the main post office on

Eighth Avenue, and they'd seen all the thousands of letters in a giant bag, waiting to get sorted and delivered. Was his letter to Lily Goldberg already waiting in Cleveland? Maybe he could call the main post office there and have someone find it and rip it up. He knew that was preposterous, but the idea made him feel a little better.

Felix kept running.

But he didn't run home.

Instead he ran to the Hotel Viking, where his father was in Room 208, probably still asleep.

"Hey, buddy," his father said as he wiped the sleep from his eyes. "Aren't you supposed to be in school?"

"I guess so," Felix said.

His father opened the door of Room 208 wider so that Felix could come inside. How could he describe how good it felt to see his father standing there in his long gray gym shorts with the faded letters RISD practically completely gone and a T-shirt, also faded, with Leonardo da Vinci's drawing of a man on the front. RISD stood for Rhode Island School of Design, which was the art college his father went to a million years ago. And that T-shirt was from the semester he spent in Florence. Those things, plus his father's particular smell of turpentine and maybe sweat and something limy, were all so familiar and comforting that Felix, as upset as he felt, broke into a grin.

"We used to call that *bunking school*," his father said.

He sat on the bed and picked up the phone beside it.

"Could you send up a pot of coffee, some chocolate milk, an eggs Benedict, bacon, and some pancakes, please?" he said to room service. He glanced at Felix. "Blueberry?"

Felix nodded, grinning even more.

His father hung up and ran his hands through his curly hair. Like Maisie's, his hair had a mind of its own.

"So you're not in school because . . . ," his father prompted.

"Dad," Felix said, sitting beside him on the bed, "is there any way to retrieve a letter from the main post office in Cleveland, Ohio?"

"No," his father said. "Once a letter is mailed, it's gone."

Felix groaned. "That's what I was afraid of."

"Why are you sending letters to Cleveland, Ohio, anyway?"

Felix flopped back on the bed and stared up at the ceiling.

His father waited.

"Lily Goldberg," he said finally.

His father waited some more.

"She's a girl," Felix added.

"Most people named Lily are girls," his father agreed.

"She moved to Cleveland and promised to stay in touch and, okay, I wasn't a very good friend, but she was in Newport this weekend and didn't even call me or anything," Felix said, his words spilling out in a rush. "And," he continued, "I wrote her a letter before I knew that."

"Ah!" his father said. "Of course, it's possible that she was only here for a day, or her parents kept her too busy—"

"Who's side are you on, anyway?" Felix asked rhetorically.

Room service knocked on the door, and his father let the guy in. He was rolling a big cart with white linen and lots of plates covered with silver lids and a white vase with a pink carnation in the middle. Felix watched his father sign for the food and then start lifting the lids, the smell of warm pancakes and bacon filling the room.

His father plucked a piece of bacon from the plate and popped the whole thing in his mouth.

"I say just wait and see what she does when she gets the letter," he said while he chewed.

Felix sniffed the little silver pitcher of maple syrup to determine if it was real or the fake stuff. He hated the fake stuff. But this smelled rich and maple-y, so he poured it over his pancakes and then carefully cut them into small even pieces. Felix didn't like large chunks of pancake.

"I say . . . ," his father said as he cut into his eggs Benedict and watched the yolk run all over the hollandaise sauce, which Felix found disgusting. "I say females are a curious species."

Felix nodded. He took a bite of his pancakes, liking the way the blueberries and maple syrup tasted together.

"Leonardo da Vinci," he said after he swallowed. "He wasn't from the Renaissance, was he?"

His father laughed. "Where did that come from?"

Felix pointed to his father's shirt.

"Ah! The Vitruvian Man."

"The what man?" Felix asked even as he took another bit of pancake.

"Vitruvian. My shirt is too faded for you to see very clearly, but basically it's based on the work of the ancient Roman architect Vitruvius. Da Vinci made a pen-and-ink drawing of a man in two superimposed images surrounded by both a circle and a square."

Felix squinted at the shirt but could only vaguely make out the man's arms and legs there.

"And, yes," his father said, "da Vinci lived during the Renaissance."

"We're studying the Renaissance in school," Felix explained.

"My favorite period," his father said.

He had polished off both halves of his eggs Benedict as he spoke, and now turned his attention to Felix's pancakes.

"Are you going to finish those?"

Felix sighed. It was easy to only think of the good things about a person when they were far away. But here was his real father, right beside him, and Felix remembered how he always ate off everyone's plate. *Insatiable*, his mother used to say, only half-kidding.

"You can have some," Felix relented, because it had been so good to be able to walk to his father for advice.

His father grinned at him, stuck his fork in one of the pancakes, and put it on his plate. Obviously, big chunks of pancake did not bother him, Felix thought as he watched his father roughly cut the pancake into fourths and begin to eat it.

"Since you've given yourself a holiday from school today," his father said, "you can come with me to take that monstrosity of a dog you and your sister brought home to the vet."

"He's going to need surgery," Felix said.

His father looked at him, surprised.

Felix shrugged. "Just a guess," he said.

Felix and Maisie's mother came home from work and a visit to Great-Uncle Thorne in the ICU looking more tired and more rumpled than usual.

"He's not getting any better," she told them as she sunk into the pink pouf in Maisie's room.

"I wish we could do something," Felix said.

"Me too," his mother said. "It's so hard to see him hooked up to all those machines, just lying there like that."

Maisie thought about how today Mrs. Witherspoon had explained that the Renaissance was a rebirth in the arts in Europe after the Dark Ages, a period that lacked, as Mrs. Witherspoon said, *Light. Intellectual, artistic, and political light.* Maybe Great-Uncle Thorne was in his own personal Dark Ages, and then he would be reborn.

"It's been a rough day," her mother said, pulling herself off the pouf. "I think I'll take a cup of tea and get in bed."

She kissed them both on the top of the head and left the room.

Felix looked at Maisie.

"You know what we have to do," he said.

"Maybe he'll be reborn," she offered.

"He will if we go up to The Treasure Chest," Felix said.

"I don't know if we should do that until we find out what happened when Hadley and Rayne found Amy Pickworth."

"What does that matter?" Felix asked. "We can't

let Great-Uncle Thorne die."

Maisie frowned, considering. Then she got an idea.

"You know how we were doing the unit on aviation and we tried to find Lindbergh?" she said, her eyes twinkling.

"So?" Felix said. He always felt a little nervous about Maisie's bright ideas.

"Well, Mrs. Witherspoon said that the Renaissance started in Florence, Italy."

"So?" Felix said again.

"Maybe we could go there. See for ourselves what it was like."

She was already heading toward the door.

Felix sighed. He knew better than to argue with Maisie. And besides, they had to save Great-Uncle Thorne, didn't they?

"We don't even have to go to The Treasure Chest," he said, reaching into his pocket.

Maisie paused, her hand on the doorknob.

"What do you mean?"

Felix reached into his pocket and pulled out the gold seal.

"I think this will get us there," he said, opening

his palm for Maisie to see. "Great-Uncle Thorne always told us we should think more about where we're going," he added.

"But . . ." Maisie hesitated.

"I thought this was what you wanted," Felix said, frustrated.

"Don't they speak Italian or Latin or something? How will we understand anybody? At least we had Pearl to translate for us in China."

Felix nodded slowly. "That's a good point," he said.

They both gazed at the gold seal with the *giglio* at the end until Felix said, "Maisie, back at the World's Fair in St. Louis, remember the Philippine village?"

"What about it?"

"Remember how all I heard was that woman speaking Tagalog, but you understood her completely? And she understood you, too?"

"That's right," Maisie said. "I wonder why."

"Did you do anything different that day before we went up to The Treasure Chest with Great-Uncle Thorne and the Ziff twins? Anything that you hadn't done before?"

Maisie shook her head. "I don't think so."

Absently, she moved the shard back and forth on

its string around her neck.

"We always do it the same way," she said.

Felix pointed to the shard.

"What's that?"

"You know. The shard from the Ming vase," Maisie said. "I put it on a string so I wouldn't lose it."

"When did you do that?" Felix asked her. "Usually it's in your pocket."

"But I didn't have a pocket. And I knew we needed the shard to travel—"

"Then that's it, Maisie! That shard allowed you to communicate!"

Maisie shook her head. "I don't think so. I had it in my pocket in China and I couldn't communicate."

"Maybe wearing it is different than having it in your pocket," Felix wondered out loud.

"If that's true, then what will happen if we get separated? You won't be able to talk to anyone, and no one will understand you. That would be a total disaster."

"I guess," Felix said thoughtfully, "that we need another shard."

"How in the world are we going to get another shard? We can't break one of the vases," Maisie said.

"I don't know," Felix admitted. "But there must be a way to do it."

"How did Great-Uncle Thorne and Great-Aunt Maisie do it?" Maisie asked. "They went to Egypt and France and everywhere. They must have both been able to communicate."

Felix looked at her.

"You're right," he said. "But how?"

CHAPTER 5

THE SECOND SHARD

Slowly, Maisie walked over to the Ming vase standing on its pedestal. There was the place where her shard fit in, she thought as she traced the hole with her finger. She slipped the thread with the shard on it over her head, and carefully placed it in its spot on the vase. And there, right above it, a small hole still remained.

"What?" Felix said, watching Maisie's face.

"Somewhere, someone had another shard," she said. "We just have to figure out who."

"And where," Felix added, staring at the hole in the Ming vase.

"Obviously, it's either Great-Uncle Thorne or Great-Aunt Maisie," Maisie said. "They must have needed it to time travel, too."

"I guess we should go into their rooms and search?" Felix said, not wanting to go into either of those bedrooms. Great-Aunt Maisie's made him sad, and now with Great-Uncle Thorne in the ICU in the hospital, it seemed wrong to snoop around his room.

"I'll take hers," Maisie volunteered. "And you can look in Great-Uncle Thorne's."

"Okay," Felix agreed, even though he got a pit in his stomach at the idea.

Resolved, Maisie put her shard back around her neck and headed toward the door.

"Wait," Felix said thoughtfully.

"Stop delaying!" Maisie said.

Now Felix walked over to the Ming vase.

"When you put your shard back, there's only *one* other piece missing," he said.

"So?"

"That means Great-Aunt Maisie and Great-Uncle Thorne only needed one shard to communicate when they time traveled."

"So?" Maisie said again, more frustrated. Sometimes Felix's cowardice was endearing. But sometimes—like now—it was maddening.

"So we already have one shard, and that's all we need," Felix explained. "What we have to figure out is how one shard lets both of us understand another language and speak it, too."

Maisie considered this. He was right. Somehow one shard worked for two people. But how?

"Maybe we have to be touching each other or something," Felix said, thinking out loud.

Maisie shook her head. "That can't be it. Remember, we spend time apart, like in China when we were separated."

"Maybe we should hold hands when we touch the object," Felix said.

Maisie winced.

"So that we'll be sure to land together," he told her, insulted.

"But what about if we get separated later?" Maisie protested. "Like in London when you were in the workhouse—"

Felix shuddered. "Don't remind me," he said.

"There has to be something we're missing," Maisie said, walking back into The Treasure Chest and staring at the small hole in the vase.

Felix stifled a big yawn. "Why don't we just

sleep on it," he suggested.

"Okay," Maisie said reluctantly, "but every minute we wait keeps Great-Uncle Thorne in that ICU."

Despite how tired Felix was, when he got into bed he couldn't sleep. He tried counting backward from one hundred. He tried deep yoga breaths, which his mother claimed always put you to sleep. He even tried naming all the states alphabetically. But all he did was get from one hundred to one, breathe a lot, real slow and deep, and name forty-four states, which left him frustrated and more awake because he couldn't figure out which six he forgot.

Warm milk, Felix thought. His father swore by warm milk. *Tryptophan*, his father claimed, even though his mother said that was an old wives' tale.

Felix got out of bed and made his way down the long hallway to the Grand Staircase. Elm Medona was definitely creepy at night. He didn't like the shadows or the way everything—clocks ticking, floorboards creaking, even his own footsteps— echoed. He walked faster, gripping the bannister as he started down the stairs.

Something caught his eye, stopping him midway.

A strange glow emanated from the wall.

Felix swallowed hard and tried to keep himself from trembling as he moved slowly toward it.

Surely it's just a trick of light or shadow, he decided.

He blinked.

No, there was definitely a glow coming from . . .

Felix stopped.

The glow emanated from the photograph of Great-Aunt Maisie as a young girl, the one where Great-Uncle Thorne stuck his head into the picture.

They both stared out at Felix, young and healthy.

Felix sighed. Up close, he couldn't see anything glowing.

But just as he turned to walk away, he saw it again. Felix reached his hand out and touched the photograph, almost expecting it to be warm.

It wasn't, of course. But what he saw was that around Great-Aunt Maisie's neck, a shard from the vase hung on a long chain. Felix peered at it. The shard was smaller than the one he and Maisie had. Maybe only half as big. But both holes in the vase were of equal size; he was sure of that.

Puzzled, Felix took a step back. His father always told him when he took him to museums to study the pictures up close and then from a distance to fully see everything.

Yes, the photograph was definitely glowing. But not around Great-Aunt Maisie, Felix saw now. The light seemed to come from Great-Uncle Thorne.

And there, around *his* neck, almost a blur, hung a shard the size of the one Great-Aunt Maisie wore.

A slow grin spread across Felix's face.

One shard. Broken into two pieces.

"You've got to wake up!" Felix said to Maisie for about the millionth time.

"Go. Away," she mumbled for about the millionth time.

"Maisie," Felix said, shaking her a little harder than was polite, "I figured it out."

"Hey!" Maisie said, and pushed him back.

"The shard," Felix said. "There's only one shard, but we need to cut it in half. You wear half and I wear the other half."

Maisie sighed, as loudly and dramatically as she could muster.

"Like those dumb lockets Bitsy Beal and Avery Mason wear," she muttered.

They got them for Christmas, two halves of a big silver heart, split down the middle. *All BFFs wear them,* Bitsy had explained to Maisie when she caught her staring at the thing. It looked like the person wearing it had a broken heart, not a BFF. But apparently when the two halves were placed together, a perfect heart appeared.

"I don't know," Felix said. "Maybe. All I do know is that once we break it in half and I get my own piece, we can go to Florence and find whoever should get the seal, and come home and save Great-Uncle Thorne."

Exhausted, he plopped down beside Maisie, who was frowning at him.

"How in the world are we going to cut the shard?" she asked. "It's porcelain. It might shatter into a *thousand* pieces, not just one."

"We'll just get a hammer—"

"A *hammer*?" Maisie said, disgusted. "That will definitely shatter it."

She was right. Hit the shard with a hammer and it would definitely break into bits.

But Felix didn't feel dejected for too long.

"Wait!" he said, sitting up. "How about one of

Mom's CUTCO knives?"

In January, a college student named Samantha had come to Elm Medona selling knives. *To help me pay for my college tuition!* she'd explained brightly.

Then Samantha had proceeded to cut all sorts of things in half with these supersharp knives: a tomato, a slab of raw steak, a piece of wood, and finally a shiny penny. Even though their mother had no need for knives at all since a very fancy set of French knives hung in the Kitchen, she was a sucker for someone with, as she called it, *gumption. I'll take the deluxe set*, she'd told Samantha, who in a flash as quick as she'd sliced that penny produced a credit-card machine and had taken their mother's American Express card. Samantha handed their mother a Y-shaped vegetable peeler and a complicated manual can opener as bonuses for buying the deluxe set. Then she was gone, and the knives had never left their polished wooden box lined with fake red velvet.

Until now.

One table in the Kitchen was lined with perfect circles of dough left by Cook to rise overnight. The air smelled yeasty but also of the strong cleaning solution that Great-Uncle Thorne insisted they use here. While Felix unearthed the knives, Maisie took the shard from her neck and wiped flour from the marble-topped counter before setting it down there.

Felix stared into the box, the knives inside all lined up against the fake red velvet, glistening. He remembered Samantha, with her blond hair held back by a hot-pink headband and her crookedly lined eyes, like she'd just learned how to put on makeup. She'd worn funny shoes, too, ugly brown ones with what his mother called *a practical heel*. And clear panty hose a shade too dark for her skin tone. *Darling*, his mother had announced as she clutched her deluxe set of knives and watched Samantha teeter off across the snowy driveway to her used green Toyota.

But which knife would do the trick now? Felix wondered. The one that so easily cut that penny? Or this bigger one that had sliced that block of wood in half? His fingers tentatively touched the skinnier one. Samantha had seemed especially proud of the way it had sliced a tomato. *But how hard was it to do that?* Felix had thought then, and thought again now. Still, his mother had gushed over that, too.

"What on earth are you doing over there?" Maisie demanded.

"Choosing the right knife for the job," Felix said, quoting Samantha.

"Just grab any one and let's go!"

Not only was Maisie tired and grumpy, but now that Felix had figured out what to do, all she could think of was Great-Uncle Thorne in that ICU. He could die at any minute!

"Hurry!" she yelled at Felix.

He appeared wielding a big shiny knife.

"It's the one that cut that penny in half," he explained.

"Whatever," Maisie said, and took the knife from him before he started to worry over exactly how to do this.

She held the knife on the shard, then paused.

"Which way?" Maisie asked.

"What?"

"Well, I could cut it longways," she said, slicing the air above the shard. "Or crossways." She sliced the air the other way to demonstrate.

"Gee," Felix said, "I don't know. I mean, the shards are so tiny in the picture. They just look equal in size."

Maisie and Felix both stared at the shard on the marble counter.

"Crossways," Maisie said.

"Longways," Felix said at the exact same time.

They looked at each other, then back at the shard.

"Crossways," Felix demurred.

Just as Maisie agreed, "Longways."

They looked at each other again.

Then Maisie took a deep breath, lifted the knife, and cut right through the porcelain shard crossways. Maybe it was a good thing that Felix had taken so long to choose the proper knife, because it slid through the shard easily, as if it were made of butter.

Really, there was no need for them to go up to The Treasure Chest. Felix had the seal in his pocket, and they both had half of the shard on yarn around their necks. But Maisie thought it would be better luck for them to leave from The Treasure Chest. For one thing, who knew if the shards would actually work the way they thought? For another, they needed luck to save Great-Uncle Thorne.

Together, Maisie and Felix pressed the spot on the wall that caused it to open. They walked, single file, up the stairs to The Treasure Chest and stepped over the velvet rope that hung across the doorway. The Treasure Chest felt oddly cold, and Maisie and Felix both shivered when they entered. Felix noticed that the stained-glass window that sent beautiful rays of light and color across the room in sunlight appeared flat and blank in the darkness.

"Ready?" Maisie asked, holding out her hand.

Felix took the gold seal from his pocket, pausing ever so slightly before he offered it to Maisie to touch. If the shard didn't work, and he got separated from Maisie, he would be in a foreign country, in a foreign time, unable to communicate or understand. If—

"Felix!" Maisie said.

Felix nodded and held the seal out for his sister to touch.

As soon as she did, he felt himself being lifted off the floor. He glimpsed Maisie, grinning as she tumbled. He smelled Christmas trees and all the wonderful smells that the wind carried on it.

Then, for an instant, nothing.

And then Felix and Maisie landed and a fair-haired, curly-headed boy was standing over them, staring wide-eyed.

"Well," he said with a smirk. "Where did you come from?"

Maisie looked at Felix and smiled.

Felix smiled back.

They had both understood the boy perfectly.

CHAPTER 6

SANDRO

The boy pointed at them and smiled, too.

"I have never seen such costumes," he said, nodding approvingly. "The Cat. The Owl. The Fool. All so common. But this—"

Here he swept his hands in a grand gesture.

"This is unique," he finished.

Felix glanced around the room. It seemed to be a laboratory or studio of some kind, with long tables covered with wood and bottles and what appeared to be a pile of hair. The smell was vaguely familiar, and although Felix couldn't quite place it, it reminded him of his father.

The boy wore what looked like tights peeking out from beneath an ankle-length robe with long flowing sleeves. Over this he wore a green jacket, and over that a stiff white apron.

Seeing Felix studying his clothing, the boy shrugged.

"I was making paintbrushes," he said.

He scooped up a handful of the coarse hair piled on the table as if in explanation.

"You're a painter?" Maisie said, her voice hopeful.

The boy puffed up his chest.

"I am indeed," he said.

He gave them a quick half bow, bending slightly at the waist.

"Sandro Botticelli," he said by way of introduction.

Maisie frowned in disappointment. Here she was all the way back in Renaissance Florence, and she meets a painter no one's ever heard of.

"Your hair," Sandro said to Maisie with a sigh, "it's beautiful."

"It is?" she said, her hands instinctively smoothing her mess of tangles.

Unruly. Out of control. A wasp's nest. She'd heard it all when it came to her hair. But beautiful? Never.

"The color," he said, peering at the top of Maisie's head, "it's natural?"

"Well, of course it's natural," Maisie said, insulted.

He nodded, unaware that she'd been insulted. Or maybe he didn't care.

"Clearly you are from the north," he said as if he were thinking out loud. "Venice, perhaps? Or Milan?"

These were obviously rhetorical questions because Sandro kept on talking without waiting for an answer, circling Maisie as he spoke.

"Here," he continued, "some women have to put dye in their hair three times a week to achieve this color. And for the face!"

He stopped circling Maisie and instead stood way too close to her, studying her face.

"For nine days they soak white beans in white wine. Then they pound the beans"—Sandro made a fist and pounded the air between him and Maisie—"and return them to the wine with goat's milk, barley, and egg whites, and they let that sit for two weeks."

He slumped his shoulders in fake exhaustion.

"Finally, they have the face water to wash their skin every day and make it pale and lovely."

Sandro gave Maisie a small smile.

"Like yours," he said softly.

Maisie felt herself blushing.

"Tell me," Sandro said, still standing close to Maisie, "does everyone where you live have this yellow hair, this pale skin?"

"Not everyone," Maisie managed to answer. She was trying to think of a boy cuter than this Sandro Botticelli, but couldn't.

Sandro slapped his hands together, breaking the spell.

"I know!" he said. "I, Sandro Botticelli, will create a mask for you!"

"A mask?" Felix asked, happy to intrude. Sandro seemed to have forgotten Felix was even in the room.

At the sound of Felix's voice, Sandro spun around to face him.

"Who are you again?" he demanded.

"Felix Robbins," Felix said. "*Her* brother."

At that, Sandro's face softened.

"Ah! The baby brother!" he said.

Maisie giggled. "Yup," she said. "He's my baby brother."

Felix glared at her, but she ignored him.

"Okay, baby," Sandro said, "I will make you a mask, too."

"A mask for what?" Felix said, frustrated.

"For Carnival!" Sandro exclaimed, as if Felix was the dumbest person he'd ever encountered. "That's why you came to Florence, isn't it? For Carnival!"

"That's why!" Maisie agreed readily.

She put herself back in Sandro's line of vision. "You'll make us both masks?" she asked.

"Absolutely!" he said.

Cool, Maisie thought. *We'll have the best masks at the fair at school.* She imagined the look on Bitsy Beal's face when she caught sight of Maisie's authentic mask, made by a real Renaissance artist.

"For now," Sandro said, "I must finish the task of completing these brushes. But perhaps after dinner we could walk?" he said, again speaking only to Maisie.

"Walk? Where?"

Sandro laughed with great enjoyment.

"That's what we do here in the evening!" he said. "We stroll. Arm in arm."

He linked his arm through Maisie's.

"Like this," he said.

Maisie swallowed hard.

"Sure," she said. "I'll walk with you."

As quickly as he'd taken her arm, he dropped it.

"I'll meet you on the San Giovanni Bridge, then?"

His eyes flickered over Felix.

"Baby brother will already be asleep, yes?" he said, his eyes twinkling.

"No," Felix grumbled.

"So," Maisie said as she watched Sandro return to his work, "what time on the San Giovanni Bridge?"

"When you hear the bell that sounds like a cow," he said. "Moo-oo!"

"The bell that sounds like a cow," Maisie repeated to herself. "Got it."

She only hoped she could wait that long. Suddenly, the idea of strolling with Sandro Botticelli sounded like the best idea she'd ever heard.

"What a pompous jerk," Felix said as soon as they stepped outside into the damp early-morning air.

"Mmmm," Maisie said, not listening. She thought he was pretty cute.

"I don't want his dumb mask," Felix said, even though he did want it. Surely it would be the best mask of the entire class.

He paused to glance around.

They were standing on a cobblestone street surrounded by stone buildings, many with balconies hanging over the street. Alleys and other streets twisted and turned everywhere Felix looked. Ahead, he could see a large plaza. Behind, an arched bridge stretched across a river that appeared green in the misty morning light.

"What shall we do with an entire day in Florence?" Felix asked, his wound from Sandro's teasing beginning to dull, and the excitement of being where they were taking hold.

Maisie didn't answer. She just stood there all dreamy-eyed.

Felix elbowed her in the ribs.

"Hey!" he said. "What do you want to do?"

She took another peek back at the building where, inside, Sandro made his paintbrushes, then sighed and shrugged.

"I don't care," she said.

"Fine," Felix said.

He pointed toward the bridge.

"Let's go that way, then."

Men had begun to fill the streets, walking in groups of three or more, heads bent together as if in very important discussion. Some of them stared at Felix and Maisie as they passed, whether because of their unusual clothing or the fact that there seemed to be no children out and about, Felix couldn't tell. But remembering his horrible time in the workhouse, and then in that terrible chimney, he worried that maybe they shouldn't be out on the street at all. But where could they take shelter?

Oblivious, Maisie stopped to watch as some men set up tables right on the street. They placed impressive boxes on top, and when they unlocked the boxes Maisie saw that they were full of money.

"Are they selling something?" she wondered out loud. But they had no goods to sell. "Or maybe giving money away?"

Felix touched her arm.

"Look," he said as a man began to count his money.

There, stamped right on the money, was the *giglio*.

"What are you children doing here?" the man asked gruffly.

He was a portly man with a big black mustache and the kind of eyebrows that look like one long caterpillar stretching over his heavy lidded eyes.

"Uh . . . um . . . ," Felix stammered, suddenly afraid they weren't supposed to be there.

"Go back home where you belong," the man

barked. "Or I'll feed you both to the lions."

With a sinister laugh, he gestured behind Maisie and Felix and then returned to arranging his money on the table.

Slowly, Maisie and Felix turned around.

There, across the small piazza, two lions paced in an ornate cage.

"Lions?" Felix managed to gasp. "Again?"

"At least these lions are locked up," Maisie pointed out.

"Still . . . ," Felix muttered.

"I don't think they really feed children to them," Maisie said.

Felix glanced at the man as he peered from beneath his unibrow.

"I'm not so sure," Felix said.

Maisie slapped his arm playfully.

"Come on," she said, not waiting for him but instead forging ahead. "Let's see what's down by the river."

Felix glanced at the lions again, a slow shiver spreading up his arms.

No problem, he said to himself.

Maisie and Felix happily wandered along the Arno River for the rest of the day. They stopped to study the goldsmiths and furniture-makers working in their shop windows, unaware of the children staring in at them. Each craftsman worked in an area filled with others doing the same work: all the goldsmiths were grouped together, all the furniture-makers. And then the feather merchants and candle-makers.

The day passed pleasantly, Maisie and Felix transfixed by the way the men shaped table legs from wood, or put fire to soft gold, or dipped the wicks into enormous pots of melted white wax to make pillar candles. A candle-maker leaving his shop offered them some bread and a chunk of smelly cheese, which they accepted readily, although Felix skipped the cheese.

As they approached the Ponte Vecchio, the harsh metallic smell of blood filled their noses. That bridge, they soon saw, was where the butchers set up shop. All kinds of raw meat hung from hooks and dripped blood in puddles along the bridge. Innards hung there, too, disgusting trails of intestines and organs that made Felix have to look away. Maisie poked him in the ribs and he glanced up just in time to see a pig's head grinning at them.

"Gross!" he said, focusing on his feet again and trying to avoid the oozing blood.

It seemed to take forever, but finally they were across the Ponte Vecchio and away from the meat and the butchers in their blood-splattered smocks.

A bell rang, low and mournful, marking the time.

"Does that sound like a cow to you?" Maisie said hopefully.

"Maybe," Felix said, remembering that they were getting to meet with that pompous Sandro Botticelli.

The bell rang again, Maisie carefully counting to check the time.

"That's definitely the one," she said. "Let's hurry!"

They moved through the thick crowd of Florentines out for an evening stroll, making their way to the Piazza della Signoria.

There, Maisie stood right in the center, scanning the people's faces for Sandro's, while Felix sulked beside her. "Let's hurry to the bridge!" Maisie shouted.

"He's probably not even coming," he finally said, relieved. "What a jerk."

"Who exactly is a jerk?" someone asked, his voice mocking.

Felix looked up, straight at Sandro standing before them. "No one," Felix said, shuffling his feet awkwardly.

"Ah!" Sandro said. "All right, then."

He linked his arm through Maisie's.

"Shall we stroll?" he asked.

Maisie could only nod.

When Felix began to walk on the other side of Sandro, Sandro halted.

"I will return her safely to this very spot at ten o'clock," he said.

"Whoa!" Felix said. "Ten o'clock? I don't think—"

But Sandro and Maisie had already moved away from him.

"Um, Maisie?" Felix called.

But his sister didn't even bother to turn around. She had her head tilted up to catch every obnoxious word Sandro Botticelli said to her.

Felix stood in the crowd in the Piazza della Signoria and watched until his sister and Sandro were nothing more than tiny specks of color in the fading Tuscan light.

CHAPTER 7

IN VERROCCHIO'S STUDIO

"**B**oy," Felix heard someone call to him, "why are you dressed that way?"

Dejected, Felix stopped walking and looked in the direction from which the voice had come.

After Maisie took off with Sandro, Felix stood in the piazza, unsure of what to do or where to go. He was tired. He was hungry. And he was angry. Eventually, he started to aimlessly wander the narrow twisty alleys of the city.

"Are you from far away?" the boy behind the voice asked.

Unlike Sandro and his mocking voice, this boy seemed genuinely curious. His eyes were dark and very intense, and he wore a thoughtful, curious expression on his face.

"Yes," Felix admitted. "Very far away."

"You are a traveler!" the boy said, impressed.

"Yes," Felix said again.

"Then you must be weary?"

Felix nodded.

"And hungry?"

"Oh, yes," Felix said.

The boy broke into a grin. "Then come inside and share my meal with me."

He opened the door wider to allow Felix to follow through it.

"It isn't much," he said apologetically. "I've been working on this painting, and I lost track of time."

Felix studied the unfinished painting, a large canvas covered with what looked like religious figures—angels and saints and the like.

"I'm satisfied with the background," the boy said, pointing to rocks jutting from a brown mountain stream.

"I don't know much about painting," Felix said, "but that looks really good. Realistic," he added.

"Yes," the boy said, his eyes still on the painting.

"My father is a painter," Felix said, feeling

homesick. "He studied here, in Florence."

"Then I must know him! With whom did he apprentice?"

Realizing what a mistake it had been to say something like that, Felix just shrugged. "It was a long time ago."

"Tell me his name," the boy said.

"Jacob Robbins," Felix said, feeling his cheeks grow warm.

The boy frowned. "I have never heard such a name. Robbins?"

"It's English, I think," Felix offered, hoping they could just change the subject.

"English?" the boy said, surprised. "Have you come from England?"

Felix shook his head. "It's complicated," he said.

The boy studied Felix's face carefully.

"Ah," he said at last, "I promised you some food, didn't I?"

He disappeared out of the room for what seemed a very long time, and Felix took the opportunity to look around the studio. The place smelled bad, like oil burning and food cooking, not a good combination. Blank canvases leaned against the wall, and drawings covered a table that reminded Felix of a drafting table. Felix picked up one of the drawings and gasped, surprised.

In pen and ink, someone—maybe this very boy?—had drawn what looked like early airplanes.

"My flying machines," the boy said, startling Felix.

"Oh," Felix said. *Flying machines? In the fifteenth century?*

"I spend many afternoons and evenings at dusk studying birds and bats," the boy said eagerly. "According to the laws of mathematics, the bird is an instrument equipped to lift off."

His hands, held together like two wings, slowly rose into the air in front of Felix.

"I say, then man has the power to reproduce an instrument like this with all its movements. What do *you* say?"

"I say yes," Felix agreed, nodding. "Absolutely."

"But how?" the boy said, studying his own drawings briefly before slapping his forehead with the palm of his hand. "Our supper!"

The room had no chairs, just benches to sit on. Felix slid onto one across from the boy, who ladled vegetable soup into a bowl for Felix, and then for himself. He slid a wooden board covered with slices of thickly cut bread in front of Felix.

"This soup is my own recipe," he told Felix. "You see, I've been a vegetarian since I was a small boy, so I often cook my own meals. I like experimenting with different herbs and spices."

Felix tasted the soup. "It's delicious!" he pronounced, and eagerly ate more, dipping the hard saltless bread into the rich broth.

"I'll give you the recipe if you like," the boy said eagerly.

"That would be great," Felix said, his mouth full of soup and bread.

"I suppose that growing up on a farm, I developed a special relationship with animals, and I can't imagine eating them."

"We have a dog," Felix said. "A big shaggy thing named James Ferocious."

The boy laughed. "Is he? Ferocious?"

"The opposite!" Felix said.

Felix watched as the boy began to eat, holding his utensil with his left hand. Felix's father was left-handed, too, and he almost commented on this similarity. But he didn't want the boy to start asking questions again, so he ate instead, in silence, savoring the delicious vegetable soup.

"I noticed that you're interested in the fact that I'm left-handed," the boy said.

Felix blushed. "Sorry I was staring."

"It's not a good trait here. Some people think it's the sign of the devil."

"Not me!" Felix protested. "My father's left-handed!"

"You know, many Florentines believe that studying the past helps with the present. But I believe we learn from observation. Like the way you were observing me," the boy continued between bites. "What theories did you come up with watching me?"

"Well," Felix said thoughtfully, "I saw that you are left-handed like my father, and since he's an artist, too, I wondered if maybe being left-handed is something many artists have in common."

The boy nodded. "Interesting," he said.

"Like you observing birds to understand their flight patterns."

"I don't just observe the flight pattern of birds. I observe all of nature. The movement of water, the arrangement of leaves on a stem. For example," he said, tapping the table, "I spend much of my time alone, in the mountains, to observe nature. There, I found fossils, shells and fish and coral, all in the mountains, far from the sea. I asked myself, *How did these get here?*"

He looked at Felix, seeming to wait for an answer.

"I don't know," Felix said. "Maybe someone brought them there?"

"Aha! Some*one*? Or some*thing*?"

Before Felix could respond, the boy said in disbelief, "Do you know that the popular theory is that these fossils floated up the mountain during the Great Flood? Which is scientifically impossible."

He shook his head. "These things are too heavy to float *up*," the boy said. "They're too heavy to float at all!"

"So, then, how did they get there?" Felix asked.

Without thinking, he helped himself to more soup. The boy didn't even seem to notice.

"The rock that formed that mountain," the boy said, his eyes ablaze with excitement at his theory, "must have once been at the bottom of the ocean. The ocean receded, leaving the fossils behind."

"Makes sense," Felix said, wishing science was

always explained so clearly.

"Not long ago," the boy said, forgetting his dinner, "I was boiling water and watching the lid on the pot jump up and down. I asked myself, *Why does a pot lid jump like that when water boils?*"

He looked at Felix expectantly.

"I think . . . ," Felix said hesitantly, trying to remember this very thing from science class. Something happened to water when it boiled. But what was it?

"I thought water must expand when it turned to steam," the boy said.

That sounded possible. "That's right, I think," Felix said.

"That's right, I *know*," the boy said, satisfied without being smug. "I made a glass cylinder, put water and a piston inside it, then brought the water to a boil and measured how far the piston rose." He leaned back slightly. "The water did indeed expand."

"Wow," Felix said, impressed.

"That is why my angel is not yet painted," the boy said, pointing at the big half-finished canvas.

"I should probably go and let you get back to work," Felix said, resisting the urge to lick his bowl.

"Where are you going?"

"Well, I have to go meet my sister," Felix said.

"And then? Where are you staying? I so enjoyed talking with you that I'd like to see you again."

Felix considered what to say. Finally, he opted to tell the truth.

"We haven't found a place to stay," he told the boy.

"But it's almost Carnival! Every room in Florence is taken!"

"We'll figure something out," Felix said.

The boy's face wrinkled with worry, but almost as quickly he brightened.

"You'll stay here!" he said.

"Here?"

"Yes, yes. Go and get your sister and bring her back here."

"Well . . ."

"And tomorrow I'll take you to the mountains," the boy said. "I have been thinking a lot about what happens when I throw a pebble into the pond there, and I have some theories I'd like to share with you."

"All right, then," Felix said, happy now. "I'll go and get Maisie and bring her back . . . Where am I exactly?"

The boy laughed. "This is the artist Verrocchio's studio. He has many apprentices, so there are always beds for more."

"Verrocchio's studio," Felix repeated.

"Ask anyone," the boy said. "He is one of the most famous artists in Florence."

He pointed again to the unfinished painting.

"That's his painting, in fact."

"But I thought *you* were painting it," Felix said, confused.

The boy laughed. "Surely your father doesn't do all of his painting himself, does he? The renowned artists have their apprentices do the work, too."

"They do?"

"Yes, yes. Of course." His eyes settled on the painting again, and he sighed.

"Thank you for letting us stay here," Felix said. "I'll be back with Maisie soon."

"Do you see that palazzo?" Sandro asked Maisie.

She looked up at the giant mansion, the light of oil lamps illuminating the windows and casting them in a golden glow.

"That is the home where the woman I love lives,"

he said with fierce intensity.

"The what?" Maisie said, just as fiercely.

"Simonetta Vespucci," Sandro hissed.

"You're in love with someone?" Maisie demanded.

"I'm in love with her, yes. But the question should be, is she in love with me?"

"How could you invite me to . . . stroll . . . if you have a girlfriend?" Maisie said, refusing to let the hot tears that had sprung to her eyes fall.

"What?" Sandro said. "Simonetta isn't my girlfriend! She's married." He added with disgust, "To a nobleman."

"You're in love with someone who's married?" Maisie said, rolling her eyes.

"Simonetta Vespucci," Sandro said, gazing longingly at one of the windows, "is the most beautiful woman in Florence. No! Florence and beyond!"

"Does she put that gross stuff with the beans and milk on her face, and dye her hair three times a week?" Maisie said, hoping he caught her sarcasm.

But Sandro seemed to have forgotten about her.

"Every night I come here and stand beneath her window, hoping for a glimpse of her. Just one glimpse is enough," he said.

"That's ridiculous," Maisie said.

"It is not!"

"You aren't going to marry her no matter how many glimpses you catch, if she's already got a husband. A rich husband at that," Maisie said, wanting to make him feel bad. He had hurt her feelings, and now she wanted to hurt his.

But Sandro only laughed.

"Married? I will never get married," he said with great assurance. "The prospect of marriage gives me nightmares. Love, on the other hand . . ."

He shrugged and sighed and gazed back up at the window.

"How long are we going to stand here, anyway?" Maisie said.

But Sandro appeared to not hear her. Instead, he took a few steps closer to the palazzo, his head tilted upward.

Maisie sighed, loud enough to be sure he heard her. But he didn't turn around. In fact, he took even more steps toward the palazzo.

Maisie followed his gaze up to the window, backlit in a yellowish glow from the oil lamps. There, a woman stood, staring out at them. Or, Maisie thought, at Sandro. Her blond hair seemed to begin far back on her head, revealing a pale white high forehead above her ivory face. She wore some kind of velvet dress with what looked like embroidery on it and long puffy sleeves.

"Simonetta," Sandro said softly.

As if she heard him, Simonetta tilted her head and smiled a small smile.

"Simonetta!" Sandro said again, louder, his arms opening wide.

Simonetta lifted one small hand and waved ever so slightly.

Sandro, bursting with joy, lifted his arms toward her as if he could hug her from this great distance.

But Simonetta slowly drew a curtain, hiding herself from him. For a moment, her shadow remained, and then it, too, disappeared.

Sandro dropped to his knees.

"Such pain!" he moaned. "She's stabbed me in the heart with that one small action."

Maisie glanced around, embarrassed. "Get up," she whispered, trying unsuccessfully to pull him to his feet.

Sandro grew even more dramatic, dropping his

head lower and banging his palms on the cobblestone street.

"Such love!" he said.

"Sandro," Maisie pleaded, "stop being so dramatic."

Slowly, he lifted his head, revealing tearstained cheeks and eyes glistening in the evening light.

"Stop?" he repeated in disbelief. "How can one stop loving the love of his life?"

"But she's married," Maisie reminded him.

She couldn't believe none of the passersby stopped to stare at this guy kneeling in the street and carrying on like this. But no one did.

"The heart doesn't understand such obstacles," Sandro said, his voice stronger. "The heart knows what it knows."

"People do stop loving the love of their lives, by the way," Maisie said, thinking of her parents. They had been so in love that she and Felix used to ask them to stop holding hands in public. Once, her father told her that when he met her mother, his heart went boom.

"Sometimes," she continued, "your heart goes boom at first, and then it just goes back to regular."

"No," Sandro said, shaking his head sadly. "I will

love Simonetta until the day I die."

"My parents said that, too," Maisie said, losing her patience with Sandro's overly romantic notions. "They promised to love each other in sickness and in health, for better or worse. But instead, they fell out of love and got divorced."

"This is terrible, Maisie!" Sandro said, jumping to his feet. His eyes glowed with great passion. "Something is wrong with what you say. Love is endless. Love is . . . eternal!"

"Then how do you explain my parents?" she said, equally passionate.

"They didn't love each other in the first place," Sandro said firmly. "That is the only explanation."

"They held hands all the time!" Maisie said, her hands on her hips as if she were preparing for a fight. "They sang together!"

Sandro pulled her hands from her hips and held them in his calloused ones.

"You must not do this," he said, looking her right in the eyes. "You must believe in love, and you must believe that no matter what happened to your parents, love is eternal."

Maisie opened her mouth to protest, but stopped.

This sounded very much like a lesson, like something she and Felix needed to know. Was the seal of the *giglio* meant for Sandro Botticelli?

She freed her hands from his and reached into her pocket, pulling out the gold seal.

"Sandro," she said, opening one of his hands and placing the seal in it, "this is for you."

Puzzled, he looked down at what she'd placed in his hand.

"What is this?" he asked.

"For letters," Maisie said. "You know, you drip hot wax on the back and then stamp it with this seal."

Sandro held the seal up closer to better examine it.

"Why would I want this?" he asked finally.

"That's the symbol of Florence," Maisie explained.

"I know what it is," he said. "I just don't need it."

He handed it back to her.

Maisie hesitated. If Sandro didn't want it, then it wasn't intended for him.

"Are you sure?" she asked.

"Absolutely," he said.

Resigned, Maisie put the seal back in her pocket.

"Shall we walk some more?" Sandro suggested.

"What about Simonetta?"

"She won't appear again, I'm afraid. I'm lucky if I glimpse her once. Twice? Impossible."

"Seriously," Maisie said as they continued along the Arno River, "you need to find a different girlfriend. Someone who isn't married, for example."

Sandro shrugged. "A heart doesn't take advice."

Maisie thought about how her mother wouldn't listen to reason about Bruce Fishbaum, and how her father almost married Agatha the Great, and how neither of them would take her advice to get married again—to each other.

"That's true," Maisie admitted.

From deep inside her stomach, a hungry growl made its way out and into the night.

"Oops," Maisie said. "I guess I haven't eaten in a long time."

"But why didn't you say so?" Sandro said. "Right here we can stop and have some meat and cheese."

He pointed to a busy shop across the street.

"The owner is my good friend Pasquale. He will let us taste a little of this, a little of that."

"I'd like a lot of something," Maisie said, which made Sandro laugh.

Inside, the shop stank of cheese, the kind her

father liked, but no one else did. She wrinkled her nose, trying not to show her disgust.

A short fat man came from around a counter of cheeses and dried meats, grinning at the sight of Sandro.

The two men hugged and gushed for so long that Maisie had to clear her throat to remind them she was there.

Sandro introduced her to Pasquale, who hugged her and gushed at her for so long that she finally said, "Nice to meet you, too," very loudly, and then, "Sandro said you might have some snacks?"

"Ah!" Pasquale said happily. "A hungry girl!"

He went back around the counter, saying in a singsong voice, "A hungry girl, a hungry girl, Pasquale loves a hungry girl."

Maisie stood on tiptoe to watch as he sliced and chopped salami and cheeses of all kinds, whistling as he placed them on a big round plate with olives and hunks of bread.

"Taste! Taste!" Pasquale said when he was done, holding the plate out to Maisie and Sandro.

She eyed the cheese, wanting to avoid the smelliest, and stuck to the salami instead. She had never seen so many different kinds of salami. There were small discs, hard red slices, softer large ones, and one studded with what looked like seeds. And each kind tasted different—salty, sharp, spicy, and even like licorice.

Sandro and Pasquale laughed as they watched her eat.

"May I have one tiny piece of salami?" Sandro teased her.

Reluctantly she let him have a few pieces, and some cheese and olives, too.

Usually, Maisie didn't like most olives, but Great-Aunt Maisie's love of Niçoise olives had made her fond of those. These were fat and green, cracked and sitting in oil and spices. And, Maisie decided as she tasted one, even better than those shrivelly black Niçoise olives.

Finally, she couldn't eat even one more bit. She'd managed to avoid the smelly cheese and nibbled on a hard buttery-tasting one instead.

"Phew," she said, wiping the oil from her mouth with the back of her hand, "I am stuffed."

"I bet you are," Sandro said. "You've eaten enough to feed a horse. Two horses!"

Then Sandro and Pasquale set about hugging each other good-bye, and then Pasquale hugged Maisie good-bye, and then finally they were back outside on the dark street.

"Felix!" Maisie said, suddenly remembering that she was supposed to meet him at ten o'clock.

"We'll go to him now," Sandro said. "We are only a little late."

Sure enough, Felix was waiting right where he was supposed to be, looking worried and anxious, pacing back and forth.

When he saw Maisie, a look of relief came over him.

"Maisie," he said, "I was afraid—"

Sandro reached down and pinched Felix's cheek.

"I was feeding her!" Sandro said. "No need to worry when she is with Sandro Botticelli."

"Ouch!" Felix said, rubbing his cheek.

"I'll have your masks ready before Carnival," Sandro promised.

"When is Carnival?" Maisie asked.

"In two days," Sandro said, confused. "You came to Florence for Carnival and you don't know when it is?"

"Um . . . ," Maisie said.

"Where are you spending *berlingaccio*?" Sandro asked.

"Um . . . ," Maisie said again.

"You will spend it with me!" Sandro declared, banging his chest. "At Lorenzo de' Medici's Palazzo Medici!"

"Okay," Maisie said.

Felix kicked her in the ankle.

"Felix too, right?" she said, glaring at Felix.

"Yes, yes, of course," Sandro said dismissively. "Felix too."

"Thank you," Maisie said, trying to remember the long *b* word he'd said, so she could find out what exactly they would be doing at this palace.

It was her turn to kick Felix.

"Right," he said on cue. "Thank you."

Sandro turned to leave, but he almost immediately turned back toward them.

"Where are you staying?" he asked Maisie.

Felix stepped forward, into Sandro's path.

"At my friend's," he said.

"Really?" Sandro said, cocking his head. "And where is your friend?"

"At Verrocchio's studio," Felix said smugly.

"Really?" Sandro said, impressed now. "I know every single artist there."

"I'm sure you do," Felix said.

"You will be in good hands," Sandro said, and once again turned to leave.

But once again he stopped and turned around.

"How do you know anyone in Verrocchio's studio?" he asked.

"Our father," Felix said quickly. "He studied art here in Florence. A long time ago," he added to avoid more questions.

Sandro nodded. "An artist," he said.

"Yes!" Maisie said, pleased that Felix had come up with an answer so quickly.

She wondered if he really had made a friend in this Verrocchio's studio, if they really did have a place to stay. The night had grown chilly, and very dark.

Sandro nodded again. "Good night, then," he said, tipping his hat slightly.

This time, he really did leave them, walking off into the night.

CHAPTER 8

LEONARDO DA VINCI

By the time Maisie and Felix got back to Verrocchio's studio, making their way through the dark streets lit here and there by candles placed in front of shrines, clouds had swept over the sky, covering the stars.

Felix's friend seemed distracted and deep in thought as he let them in. The smock he wore had spots of paint on it, and his hands were streaked with various shades of blue paint. He led them to a small storeroom and gave them each a heavy blanket and small flat pillow.

"In the morning, we will go to the hills," he said to Felix. "But tonight . . ."

He gave a little apologetic smile and a shrug before leaving them there with a lit oil lamp.

"Friendly," Maisie muttered.

"He is friendly," Felix insisted. "He's just busy finishing a painting."

Maisie yawned.

"Not that I feel like staying up and chatting," she said, wrapping the blanket around herself and settling onto the floor.

"Ugh," she groaned. "This is a hard floor."

Felix lay down beside her, yawning too. "What a day," he murmured.

But Maisie was already asleep, her hair spread out like a fan around her head, and her arms flung out of the blanket.

A flash of lightning lit the small room, forcing Felix to sit bolt upright.

Oh great, he thought. *A thunderstorm.*

Even at home he didn't like thunderstorms. When he was little, his mother used to tell him thunder was angels bowling. Maisie would roll her eyes at that explanation, but it made him feel a little less frightened. Now that he knew that wasn't true, thunderstorms had become scary again. And here he was back in the 1400s, which made it even—

Crack!

Thunder boomed, shaking the building.

Felix took cover under the blanket while Maisie snored lightly beside him.

Before long, another bolt of lightning lit the sky outside. Felix remembered that if he counted the time between the lightning and thunder, he would know how far away the storm was.

One, he began.

Two.

"Felix!" someone called. "Felix, where are you?"

"Under here," Felix said softly.

The blanket got torn from him, revealing his painter friend looking down at him with excitement.

"This is no time for sleep," he said.

"I wasn't exactly sleeping," Felix said.

More thunder crashed around them.

Felix ducked under the blanket again as the boy clapped his hands in delight.

"What are you doing here?" Maisie grumbled sleepily.

"Did you hear that?" the boy asked her.

"The thunder?"

"When I throw a pebble in a pond, I noticed that waves form in a circle around it," he continued, "expanding steadily outward from it."

"Okay," Maisie said. "Sure."

She yawned again. "What time is it, anyway?"

"From this observation," the boy went on, "I deduced that sound and light must also travel in waves. But through the air."

"Sound waves," Maisie said. "Right."

A bolt of lightning seemed to land right outside the house, and for a split second everything was illuminated: Maisie's sleepy face and golden hair frizzy with static electricity, Felix peeking out from beneath the blanket, and the boy grinning.

"Wait!" the boy practically shouted. "I *always* see lightning *before* I hear thunder. Yes?"

"I . . . I don't know," Maisie said. "I guess so."

"Therefore light waves must travel faster than sound waves!"

As if on cue, more thunder sounded, causing the boy to laugh with delight.

"Why is this so exciting, anyway?" Maisie said.

He looked at her, surprised.

"Discovery is the most exciting thing of all," he said.

"Are you a scientist?" she asked, frowning up at

him. "I thought you were a painter."

He shrugged. "I love nature," he said, as if that explained everything. "I learned this from my uncle Francesco. He ran my grandfather's farm about twenty miles from here, where I lived as a boy. There, we had vineyards and olive trees, and we grew wheat. My uncle would take me outdoors with him, from the time I was five or so, and I grew to love watching the birds in flight, the flowers, all of nature. From this, we learn, yes?"

Rain began to fall, hard, outside.

"But how did you learn to paint?" Felix asked, feeling safer now that the rain had come.

"I always loved to draw," the boy said. "And I was always very good at it."

Felix wondered why, if Sandro Botticelli had said that very thing, he would have sounded boastful, but this boy did not.

"One day, a local peasant made a round shield and asked my father to get it painted for him. My father immediately thought of me for the job, because he knew I could draw. Immediately I imagined painting Medusa on the shield."

"Medusa?" Maisie asked through a yawn.

"The creature with snakes in its hair, right?" Felix asked eagerly.

The boy nodded. "Exactly. I had seen many interpretations of Medusa, always looking so serene and pleasant. But I thought Medusa should be grotesque. I mean, a head full of snakes is grotesque, isn't it?"

He didn't wait for a reply. The memory had made him grow excited, and he paced as he described what he did next.

"I wanted these snakes to be realistic, not interpretive. To draw my Medusa, I needed models, so I went outdoors to collect specimens. Not just snakes, but lizards, too. What does a reptile's scale really look like? How do I capture it realistically? I positioned my models around the room where I was painting the shield, and lost myself there for many days. I'm not sure if my father screamed at the sight of Medusa, or at the smell of those dead reptiles. But when he came in, he screamed!"

Maisie wrinkled her nose at the thought of decomposing animals, but Felix grinned as he imagined such a Medusa.

"Did the man like what you painted?" Felix asked.

The boy laughed.

"My father thought it was so good that he sold it to an art dealer, and the art dealer sold it to the duke of Milan, and now here I am! In a famous artist's studio!"

"Wow," Felix said in admiration.

The sound of footsteps nearing made the three of them look in that direction.

A short, pudgy, stern-looking man appeared in the doorway.

"Aren't you working on the angel?" he said to the boy.

"I am, yes. But I noticed something important."

He held up a small notebook and opened it, revealing the strangest handwriting Felix had ever seen. The letters seemed to be written backward, and ran from right to left instead of from left to right. Once, Felix and Maisie's parents gave them a spy kit for Christmas, and one of the codes in it looked just like this handwriting. To break the code, Maisie had figured out, they just had to hold the message up to a mirror, where it became readable in the reflection.

"And I had to record it," the boy was explaining.

The man sighed. "That's all well and good," he

said, frustrated, "but did you get the paints mixed?"

"I . . . hmmm . . . I started to," the boy said, thinking hard. "I spent all morning washing and grinding the minerals—"

"Such as?" the man continued impatiently.

"Iron," the boy said. "And maybe *terra verte*?" he added uncertainly.

"And?" the man pressed. "Did you at least get it mixed with the oil and milk?"

"That," the boy admitted, "I did not do."

The man sighed again. "Why do you have so much trouble finishing things? Such a talented young man, but you get so distracted."

"Yes, Signor Verrocchio, I do get distracted. But these distractions, as you call them, are important. For example, today I was preparing to add the oil and milk, just as you ordered. But I began to think of how I could make the colors less saturated."

"Less saturated," Signor Verrocchio said in the voice of a man losing his patience.

"Exactly! Subtler! Lighter!" the boy's face beamed with enthusiasm. "Perhaps, with your permission, of course, I'll try this tomorrow?"

"Tomorrow, you will paint the angel. Or the

landscape, as my master sketches show," the artist said seriously.

"Yes, yes, of course. But first, perhaps I can add some beeswax and water when the pigment and linseed oil are at the boiling stage? To see if my theory is correct?"

The man shook his head. "Where do you get these ideas, Leonardo?"

"Leonardo!" Maisie gasped.

"Da Vinci?" Felix ventured.

"You know me?" Leonardo asked, confused.

"We . . . I mean . . . yes . . . ," Felix stammered.

"From . . . Sandro," Maisie offered.

"Ah!" Leonardo said, satisfied.

Maisie and Felix couldn't do anything except stare at him, the boy who would grow up to paint the *Mona Lisa* and *The Last Supper*, now just an apprentice mixing paint for Andrea del Verrocchio.

Maisie did not want to go up into the hills with Leonardo.

"But he's Leonardo *da Vinci*," Felix said to her in disbelief. How could anyone, even his sister, Maisie, not want to spend every possible minute with the actual Leonardo da Vinci?

"I want to see what Sandro is doing for my mask," Maisie said.

Even though she realized that Sandro stupidly loved a married woman, and was actually much older than she'd thought (he must be at least twenty, she'd decided), she didn't care. She had, she realized, a great big crush on the curly-haired, unknown painter. Someone else, like maybe Bitsy Beal or Avery Mason, would have developed a crush on Leonardo, who, with his long eyelashes and dark eyes, was what those girls would call *dreamy*. But to Maisie, Sandro was cuter and more fun to be around than someone who got all excited about light traveling faster than sound.

"Sandro Botticelli isn't even that good a painter," Felix said.

"How do you know? You haven't seen his work."

"No one's ever heard of him," Felix said.

"Apparently," Maisie said, defending Sandro, "everyone here has heard of him. He's apprenticed with some famous monk named Flippy Lippy, or something."

Felix shook his head. "Flippy Lippy? That does not sound like anyone serious about anything."

"I don't know who the guy is, but Sandro said it like he was someone very important," Maisie said.

"That's because he's a braggart!" Felix exclaimed.

"Plus," Maisie continued, deciding to ignore her brother's insult, "he's good friends with these Medici people, and apparently they run the whole city of Florence."

"Fine," Felix said. "I give up."

"Besides," Maisie said, "we're going to all go to that palace later for the . . . What did he call it?"

"*Berlingaccio*, I think," Felix said. "Whatever that is."

They were interrupted by the sound of boisterous laughter coming from the artist's studio where Leonardo had gone to paint.

"That sounds like Sandro," Maisie said happily, and before Felix could roll his eyes at her she was out the door.

Reluctantly, Felix followed.

Sure enough, Sandro stood leaning against the wall, watching as Leonardo frowned at the giant canvas. In Leonardo's hand was a clay model of an angel.

"My friend Leonardo here believes the best way to paint something is from a three-dimensional model," Sandro said, tilting his chin toward the angel.

"That makes sense," Felix said.

"Do you know how much time he spent making that clay figure instead of painting?" Sandro said, followed by more boisterous laughter. "And do you see those lines drawn on the canvas?"

Felix and Maisie peered at the canvas, following Sandro's pointing finger.

"Yes," Maisie said.

"Do you see how my friend Leonardo decided to *not* follow those lines and is doing his own design there?"

"The landscape needs sunlight!" Leonardo exclaimed. "And shadows! When you go outside, that is what you see."

"But Andrea del Verrocchio did not draw in these shadows and this sunlight, and you are his apprentice, Leonardo. That means you learn from him, not the other way around."

"That reminds me," Leonardo said, wandering away from the canvas. "I was going to finish making some red chalk. But why did I need it?"

He stared down at the clay angel in his hand as if he didn't know where it had come from.

"Ah, well, enough work for today, then," he said finally. "I believe I'll go into the hills before we meet at the palace."

"I'm coming, too," Felix said. "Remember?"

Leonardo looked as if he didn't remember, but he smiled and agreed that Felix should indeed come along.

When Sandro and Maisie were alone in the studio, Sandro pointed to a figure on the canvas.

"I painted that," he said proudly.

"Nice," Maisie said.

"Yes, I apprenticed here, too. All the great ones do," Sandro added, matter-of-factly.

"Hmmm," Maisie said, because the figure Sandro painted didn't look any better than anything else on the canvas. In fact, the rocks and ground that Leonardo had painted with shadows and light were the best part of the painting. Maisie decided to keep this opinion to herself, though.

"Would you like to see your mask?" Sandro asked her.

"You finished already?" Maisie said, delighted and surprised.

"What you will learn very quickly," Sandro said, "is that the difference between Leonardo and me is that I actually finish what I start."

An image of the *Mona Lisa* from one of her father's art books floated into Maisie's mind.

"Oh," she said, "I suspect that Leonardo will get around to finishing a painting or two."

Sandro placed a hand on her shoulder, patting sympathetically.

"One can only hope," he said.

He turned her toward the door and led her out of Verrocchio's studio, down the cobblestone alley to Fra Lippi's, where Sandro apprenticed.

There, on a long table covered with dishes of paint and boxes of chalk and paintbrushes, sat a beautiful white-and-gold mask.

"Yours," Sandro said, lifting it gently.

The gold formed intricate designs around the border, shining brightly against the pure white. He placed the mask over Maisie's eyes and nose, adjusting it until it sat just right.

"A peacock feather, perhaps," Sandro murmured as he studied it from a few steps away from Maisie.

Maisie wished there was a mirror so she could admire herself.

As if he knew exactly what she was thinking,

Sandro said, "Wait!" and retrieved a mirror from another room. He held it up for her to see.

"It's beautiful!" she gasped.

"Yes," Sandro said, "it is. The gold picks up the gold highlights in your hair perfectly, just as I thought it would."

"Do you think you'll be able to finish Felix's in time?" Maisie asked.

"It's completed," Sandro said. The corners of his mouth twisted up into a small satisfied smile.

He walked across the room to another table and lifted a terrifying mask up for Maisie to see. It looked almost like a bird, with a long beak, but sinister somehow.

"How do you like it?"

"It's . . . interesting?" Maisie offered.

Felix was *not* going to wear that, she thought. At Halloween, he always opted for gentle costumes, like a friendly ghost or the Lone Ranger, instead of vampires, skeletons, or werewolves. This thing would not suit him. At all.

"Il Medico della Peste," Sandro said. "The Plague Doctor."

"What plague?"

Sandro looked at her in disbelief.

"The plague that wiped out a third of Europe!"

"Oh," she said, not knowing what he was talking about. "*That* plague."

"Yes, *that* plague," Sandro said. "The doctors wore disguises so no one would know who had tended to the people stricken with the Black Death."

That made the mask even worse, Maisie decided.

Still, she thought, staring at her own reflection in the mirror Sandro had left on the table, her mask did pick up the golden highlights in her hair, just like he'd said. She smoothed her unruly curls and smiled at her reflection, satisfied.

In the hills above Florence, Felix and Leonardo lay on their backs in the grass, watching birds fly above them.

"If a man had a tent made out of linen," Leonardo said thoughtfully, "perhaps twenty feet across and twelve feet long—"

"A tent?" Felix interrupted, trying to picture such a thing.

"Yes! With all of the apertures stopped up, I believe he would be able to throw himself off any great height and float to the ground without sustaining any injuries."

"Oh!" Felix said. "You mean like a parachute?"

Leonardo propped himself on one elbow and looked down at Felix.

"Parachute," he repeated.

"Well, I think they're made out of silk, not linen, but, yeah, that sounds like a parachute."

"But they don't exist," Leonardo said, searching Felix's face in a way that made Felix squirm.

"Right," Felix said.

"How did you know what I was explaining?" Leonardo asked.

For reasons Felix could not understand, he said, "Because I'm from the future."

This news did not appear to surprise Leonardo.

"I wondered," he said softly. "Your clothing. Some of the things you've said . . ."

Felix met Leonardo's steady gaze.

"And my idea, this . . . parachute . . . it exists? And it works?"

Felix nodded.

"Then you must know . . . Is the moon covered with water?" Leonardo asked him eagerly.

"No, there's no water on the moon. It's just rocks," Felix said.

"But then, how does the moon reflect the light of the sun if not from the water on the moon?"

Leonardo looked so disappointed that Felix said, "But maybe there was water there a million years ago."

"What about whirlybirds?" Leonardo asked.

"I—"

"And flying machines?"

"Yes—"

"And is there a lens that helps you to see these things? The sun and the moon—"

"A telescope," Felix said.

Leonardo stared at Felix.

"Take me with you," he said.

"With me where?"

"To the future," Leonardo said simply.

CHAPTER 9

INSIDE THE PALAZZO MEDICI

Maisie and Sandro arrived at the Palazzo Medici right at the appointed hour.

"Let's hope Leonardo remembers to come," Sandro had said mockingly to Maisie when they showed up at Verrocchio's studio to find Leonardo and Felix gone.

Even though Maisie had thought they should wait, Sandro convinced her that Leonardo lived on his own terms. "He's always late, or forgets altogether, or simply decides to follow one of his harebrained theories instead of doing whatever he's supposed to be doing. Trust me, we could miss the entire party if we decide to wait."

Reluctantly, Maisie agreed.

And now that they were walking across the street that led to the palace, all thoughts of Felix vanished from her mind. Although the Palazzo Medici didn't look like a typical one—she couldn't help but imagine it would resemble Cinderella's castle in Disney World—it was a grand, imposing, enormous thing in the shape of a cube. The sight of it as it came into view made her gasp and pause to take it in. Much larger than Elm Medona, with men on horseback and uniformed guards standing sentry, the Palazzo Medici was maybe the grandest thing Maisie had ever seen.

"What do these Medicis do, anyway?" Maisie asked Sandro when she finally got her voice back.

"That is a complicated question," Sandro answered. "Lorenzo's grandfather, Cosimo, was a banker originally. A banker who eventually led the Republic of Florence. Now, the Medicis are one of the wealthiest and most powerful families in Europe."

A young man dressed all in crimson came out of the large palace entry doors. He had, Maisie thought, a ridiculous haircut. His black hair was styled into a pageboy, complete with straight bangs hanging right above his jet-black eyes.

Just as Maisie was about to ask if this was the court jester, Sandro opened his arms and said in a boisterous voice, "Lorenzo the Magnificent!"

Phew! Maisie thought, relieved that for once she hadn't embarrassed herself.

Sandro and Lorenzo set about hugging and kissing each other's cheeks, the way all the men here greeted each other.

"Am I the first to arrive?" Sandro asked when they finally separated.

"Not quite," Lorenzo said.

"Well," Sandro said conspiratorially, "I know I'm not the last to arrive."

Lorenzo laughed heartily. "That distinction always goes to Leonardo," he said.

"So, who has beaten me here?" Sandro asked.

Maisie saw how competitive he was, his eyes peering over Lorenzo's shoulder, searching for the more punctual artist.

"Piero della Francesca is, of course, here—"

"What?!" Maisie blurted.

The two men looked at her, surprised.

"Piero della Francesca is my art teacher's favorite artist," she said. "He's here?"

Lorenzo narrowed his eyes at her. "Who did you say this was, Sandro?"

"Maisie Robbins," Sandro said. "Her father studied here. Who did you say he apprenticed with?"

Thankfully, before Maisie came up with an answer, Lorenzo said, "Ah! So he knew Piero?"

"No," Maisie said, immediately regretting her honesty. "But, I mean, isn't Piero della Francesca kind of famous?"

"Someday, I hope," Lorenzo said ruefully. "As his benefactor, I believe that someday the world will know who he is."

He glanced at Sandro, who was sulking beside him.

"And Sandro Botticelli, too, of course," Lorenzo added.

"Of course," Sandro said.

They walked through the doors and into a large courtyard. The smell of the oil burning in the lamps mixed with the smells of food cooking, which made for a heavy, unpleasant aroma filling the air. Lorenzo left them to meet more guests, squeezing Sandro's shoulder as he walked past.

Although Maisie's stomach rolled at the smells,

she hardly noticed. She was standing in perhaps the most beautiful courtyard ever built, which was decorated with gold and fine marble, carvings and sculptures, and even the benches and the floor itself were made of inlaid jewels and stones. A long table was set for a feast, reminding Maisie of the Dining Room at Elm Medona, with its heavy silver and candelabras and gold plates.

Four thick marble columns supported three soaring arches that were lined with twelve oval medallions alternating a coat of arms—the Medicis', Maisie assumed—with mythological figures that she recognized from paintings and murals at Elm Medona.

"This reminds me of home," she whispered.

Sandro looked surprised.

"Does home have something like this?" he asked, pointing to a marble bust.

Maisie shrugged.

"That is an antique bust of the emperor Hadrian, restored by none other than Filippo Lippi."

"At Elm Medona," Maisie said, "we have so many sculptures and tapestries and—"

"Follow me," Sandro said, already walking ahead of her toward a small door.

Almost casually he pointed at a sculpture. "That bronze David is by Donatello," he said, sounding like a stern teacher.

As she hurried to follow, Maisie looked up at the medallions that lined the walls. One of them was very familiar.

"I've seen that before," she said, pointing.

Sandro did not even slow down. "Not unless you've been at the Palazzo Medici before," he said dismissively.

Sandro opened the small door and beckoned her inside.

She took a step in and had to stop. Maisie was standing in what appeared to be a gorgeous, lush painting. There were more busts like the one of the emperor that Sandro had pointed out. But it was the plants, all so different from each other and so exotic-looking, that took her breath away.

"It doesn't seem real, does it?" Sandro asked, his voice hushed with wonder.

"I feel like—"

"—like you've walked into a painting, yes?"

He didn't wait for her to reply.

"That's the effect Lorenzo wanted," he said.

The sounds of voices and laughter floated in the air around them.

"Everyone must be here," Sandro said. "It's time for the *berlingaccio*."

"What exactly is the *berlingaccio*?" Maisie asked.

"The eating and drinking that begins Carnival," Sandro said. He smiled. "It will be a very long night."

Reluctantly, Maisie left the garden, walking back through the small door into the courtyard behind Sandro.

There, Lorenzo stood as if holding court, surrounded by many men. Maisie searched the crowd, but Felix and Leonardo were not among them.

"Piero della Francesca," Sandro whispered in her ear, "in whom you took so much interest."

She followed his gaze to a man who looked as ordinary as any of them in the circle.

"The Pollaiuolo brothers," Sandro said, moving around the circle. "Andrea del Verrocchio—"

"Yes!" Maisie said, recognizing the man who had come into the room during the thunderstorm last night.

"Domenico Ghirlandaio . . . Marsilio Ficino . . ."

"But who are these men?" Maisie asked.

"Artists, thinkers," Sandro said, moving to join the circle. "They make up the court of Lorenzo the Magnificent."

Maisie hung back a moment, taking in the sight of the court of Lorenzo the Magnificent, lit in an amber glow. There were times, like this one, when she had the strong urge to stay in the past. The complications of home seemed far away, and this life here in the Renaissance, filled with artists and dukes and all sorts of wonder, seemed more interesting and exciting.

She fingered the seal in her pocket. This wasn't the first time she'd considered keeping it to herself. Maisie knew that at some point soon, like always, Felix would get homesick and want to return. But if she didn't have the seal . . .

Glancing around the courtyard, Maisie saw a large terra-cotta urn, its handles shaped like twisting figures along each side. She walked over to it and casually dropped the seal inside, listening with satisfaction as it landed with a pleasing *plink!* Then she moved into the circle of men.

As soon as Maisie arrived, one of the men frowned, a look of worry crossing his face. He stepped away from everyone, staring hard at Maisie.

"You—" he said, pointing at her, even though Lorenzo was talking.

Everyone became silent, and turned to also stare at Maisie.

"You are . . . ," The man paused, his eyebrows now shooting upward. "Dangerous . . ."

"It's the night before Carnival," Piero said. "You've already put a damper on the evening by telling us right off that it was an inauspicious date for a gathering. Now you're picking on our poor young visitor."

"I only say what is in the stars," Signor Ficino said. "And the stars tell me that there is trouble tonight."

"I'm not bringing any trouble," Maisie said.

Signor Ficino glared at her.

"You are . . . ," he said again. "You are . . . other!"

A woman's voice cut through the ominous pronouncement.

"Yes, Signor Ficino," the woman said, gliding through the courtyard in a heavily embroidered red dress. "She is *other*. We're called women, in case you didn't know."

The men laughed in embarrassment.

Except Signor Ficino.

He continued to stare at Maisie with a combination of horror and curiosity.

"Clarice!" Lorenzo said, taking the woman's hand in his and kissing it as he bent into a dramatic bow.

Up close, Clarice had the strangest shade of yellow hair—not blond, but yellow—and a high forehead that showed tiny dots where hair had been plucked from its natural beginning to way back on her head. Overall, the look, combined with a pasty-white face covered in powder, was creepy. But when Clarice smiled at Maisie, she softened a bit, and Maisie realized that Clarice was only a little older than her. And already married!

"My husband has the oddest friends," Clarice whispered to Maisie with a giggle, as she kept her hand drooping in the air and one by one each man bent to kiss it.

Except Signor Ficino.

He did not take his eyes from Maisie.

"Leonardo?" Clarice said, glancing at the people gathered.

"Late," Sandro answered.

"I so wanted him to play his lute for me," Clarice said with a small pout. "And to sing me a song."

"Perhaps after dinner," Lorenzo said.

Clarice sighed. "I suppose I have no choice."

To Maisie's surprise, Clarice took her hand.

"You will sit next to me," Clarice announced. "And you can tell me how you got such beautiful hair and skin."

Maisie smiled as she and Clarice walked hand in hand to the banquet table.

But Signor Ficino grabbed her by the shoulder, pressed his lips to her ear, and whispered, "*Where* are you from?"

Startled, Maisie yanked away from his grip.

"I will find out," he said coldly.

Clarice laughed. "He's full of doom and gloom," she said, tugging Maisie along again. "He's an astrologer, and he's always saying dire or ridiculous things. He told me I would have *ten* children! And he told my poor brother-in-law that he would be murdered right in the piazza!"

"That is pretty gloomy," Maisie agreed.

But Clarice was already smiling—and changing the subject happily.

"I just love *berlingaccio*, don't you?" she said, letting a servant pull back one of the heavy chairs, and sitting with a bounce.

Maisie nodded and smiled back at Clarice, but she couldn't help but notice Signor Ficino watching her.

"I don't understand," Leonardo said sadly to Felix. "Explain more clearly why I can't come with you to the future."

The sky above Florence had turned from blue to lilac to lavender, now an inky blue studded with stars.

"There are rules," Felix said, struggling to explain. "For one, you have to be a Pickworth."

"What is this Pickworth?"

"It's our name. Like yours is da Vinci," Felix said.

Leonardo frowned. "So you are from Pickworth?"

"Well, no. I mean, kind of," Felix said. "Pickworth was our great-great-grandfather's name. And probably his father's name, and so on."

"But da Vinci simply means that I am from the village of Vinci. You are not from the village of Pickworth?"

"Honestly," Felix sighed, "I have no idea. In the future, we don't do it that way."

"Well, suppose I become a Pickworth—"

"No, no," Felix protested, "it doesn't work that way. And even if it did, you have to be a twin to time travel."

"Why?"

Felix shrugged. "I have no idea."

He remembered how he'd gone to The Treasure Chest and tried to take Lily Goldberg with him, and how it had failed. Even the thought of Lily Goldberg sent a sharp pain of embarrassment through him. Had she received that letter? Did she find him pathetic?

"What else?" Leonardo was asking.

"We go into this room called The Treasure Chest," Felix said, happy to *not* think about Lily Goldberg, "and we take an object—"

"What does that mean?"

"The Treasure Chest is full of . . . of stuff. Scrolls and coins and precious jewels and feathers and crowns and maps and test tubes and compasses and . . . seals . . ."

He looked at Leonardo's expectant face. If Felix had that seal, he would give it to him right now. But Maisie had it.

"That's how we got here," Felix said. "With a seal of the city of Florence. And we need to give it to you."

"Fine, then," Leonardo said. "Give it to me. Maybe then I can come back to the future with you."

"No," Felix said, shaking his head. "Once we give it to you, we'll go back. Just Maisie and me."

"Impossible!" Leonardo said vehemently. "There must be a way!"

"Actually, that's not exactly right," Felix said. "We give you the seal, and you give us advice."

"What kind of advice?" Leonardo said. "I have no advice for you. Or for anyone."

"Not so much advice," Felix said, "but like a lesson. Something that will help us when we go back."

A slow grin spread over Leonardo's face.

"Excellent," he said. "Then I will be sure *not* to give you any lessons. Until I figure out how to return with you."

"No!" Felix said adamantly. "We need to go home. We have a family and school and . . ."

"And?"

"It's complicated," Felix said.

Leonardo waited.

"Our great-uncle, he's dying. But by time traveling, we can save his life."

"How?"

Again Felix struggled. "I don't really understand it," he said, "but every time we time travel, he gets . . . not younger . . . but healthier? More vital."

"So if you don't go back?"

"He'll . . ." Felix's voice caught. "He'll die."

"I will take this under consideration," Leonardo said finally. "Is the life of this uncle of yours more important than seeing what the future holds?"

He stood.

"We are late, and Lorenzo and the rest of them will assume I've forgotten the *berlingaccio*."

Felix stood, too.

"Leonardo," he said, "you belong here. Your ideas need to grow from this place, this time. The Renaissance—"

Leonardo interrupted. "Renaissance? Rebirth?"

Felix nodded. "That's what this era will be called. The Renaissance. A rebirth of ideas and art after the Dark Ages."

"Renaissance," Leonardo said to himself. "I like it."

When Leonardo and Felix arrived, the multicourse dinner of soup and pasta and meat and cheese had finished. The servants were just putting several ring-shaped cakes on the table for dessert.

"Ah!" Leonardo said after everyone had greeted him. "We didn't miss the *berlingozzo*!"

"Almost," Sandro kidded.

Maisie tried to make eye contact with Felix, but he had his worried look on his face, and she couldn't get past that.

The cake tasted like lemons and sugar, and Maisie happily accepted a second piece once she'd finished her first. But Felix merely moved the crumbs around on his plate.

"Come," Leonardo told him quietly, "there's something I want to show you."

They easily slipped away from the others and walked up the stairs to the family's quarters.

"You know," Leonardo said as they walked past giant tapestries, endless bookshelves that seemed to stretch forever, and more marble and gold than Felix had seen in any of the Newport mansions. "If you are alone, you belong entirely to yourself. If you are accompanied by even one companion, you belong only half to yourself. With that many people, even less."

Felix brightened. That sounded important, like a lesson. Maybe Leonardo had inadvertently told him something important, the very thing he and Maisie needed to go home.

"Here," Leonardo said, opening a door.

Felix gazed at the room. It looked like a church, complete with an altar. But it was the most beautiful church he'd ever seen.

"The Magi Chapel," Leonardo said, his voice hushed. "Frescoed by Benozzo Gozzoli."

Felix took in the frescoes that covered the walls. He recognized the scene of the Three Wise Men, but . . .

"Hey!" he said.

Leonardo laughed. "That's right. The Wise Men are the Medicis."

Felix recognized Lorenzo, with his black pageboy haircut and dark eyes.

"That's his brother, Giuliano, and his father, the two other Wise Men. The other characters are various emperors," Leonardo explained.

Felix nodded appreciatively.

From down in the courtyard, a sudden burst of voices and shouting rose up to them.

"Don't worry," Leonardo said, "they are just in the spirit of Carnival."

Almost as soon as Felix and Leonardo left, Lorenzo stood and recited a poem. It seemed to be about life and happiness but also about how those things can change so easily.

Sandro watched Maisie's face intently as Lorenzo recited.

"How can it be?" he asked softly.

Maisie turned her attention away from Lorenzo and toward Sandro.

"How can you understand Tuscan?" he asked her.

"I was wondering the same thing," Signor Ficino said.

"Tuscan is Italian, isn't it?" Maisie asked as she fingered the shard hanging cool against her skin.

"No," Sandro said, narrowing his eyes. "Tuscan is the language here, little used now. That is why I wonder how you can understand it."

"They don't speak Tuscan anywhere but in Tuscany," Signor Ficino said in that cold voice of his.

"Well," Maisie said.

"Yes?" Sandro asked expectantly.

"I'm a linguist."

Sandro frowned.

"A linguist!" Maisie repeated. "I speak so many languages I can't even name them all."

"But Tuscan?" Signor Ficino said.

Before she could answer, the front door burst open and a dozen men infiltrated the courtyard, wielding large swords and screaming, "Revenge!"

The men around the table, along with Lorenzo's new wife, Clarice, and Maisie, jumped to their feet and dispersed, some running through the small door to the garden, some running up the stairs to the family's quarters.

The intruders slashed at the air with their swords, cutting down the middle of the table, sending glass and food spraying everywhere.

Maisie stood, paralyzed.

Where was Felix?

But she had no time to think. The intruders, their faces covered in black hoods, their dark robes flapping as they set about smashing everything on the table, were in a frenzy, their swords slicing the air wildly.

She needed to get away.

One sword came so close to her that she actually heard the *whoosh* it made as it flew past. Her fingers shot up to her neck. Close? No. It had actually nicked her. Two small dots of blood were on her finger where she'd touched her neck.

Her heart pounding in her ears, Maisie dropped to the floor unnoticed and slithered under the table, watching as the men's black boots moved frantically back and forth.

"We should go upstairs and murder the lot of them!" an angry male voice said.

The men murmured in agreement.

"All in good time," another man said. "We've let the Medicis know that the Pazzis mean business."

Someone laughed a laugh so evil that the hairs on Maisie's arms stood up.

"At least let's take a souvenir," the first man said.

Maisie heard them marching around the courtyard, trying to decide which painting to take with them.

Finally, they left in as much noisy chaos as they'd arrived.

Maisie stayed beneath the table for a few minutes after the courtyard grew silent.

When she believed they were truly gone and not returning, she slid on her belly along the marble floor and emerged from beneath the table. Her heart was still pounding, so much so that she didn't hear the small sound of something dropping to the floor as she stood. She touched her neck again and found tiny drops of fresh blood there.

I've been wounded by a sword! Maisie thought, with some pride.

She wished she knew where Felix was so that she could show him, and maybe brag a little about her bravery. She had been brave, she decided. Standing amidst all those slashing swords, hiding under the table, emerging safe but bloody. The story grew even as she stood there, waiting for someone to come downstairs.

Eventually, she gave up.

Maisie had had enough excitement for one day, she decided. She would go back to Verrocchio's studio and wait for Felix and Leonardo to return. By then, her story would be even grander.

CHAPTER 10

NON CAPISCO

Maisie went to sleep alone that night, Felix and Leonardo still not yet home. She woke the next morning alone again, but the blankets beside her were tangled and messy, so Felix had come back eventually. But he had already gone off again. *Probably with Leonardo to prove some scientific theory or another*, Maisie thought with a sad sigh.

She made her way through the studio, empty except for the canvases leaning against the walls and the tables lined with painting supplies.

"Hello?" Maisie called, her voice echoing ever so slightly.

No one answered.

Of course, she realized, today was the first day of

Carnival. Everyone had gone off to watch jousting and parades.

Her mood shifted immediately from lonely to angry. Couldn't Felix have woken her up? How dare he just leave her alone while he went to see jousting. Or whatever.

Her stomach growled, reminding her that in addition to being angry, she was also hungry.

In the sunny kitchen, Maisie found half a loaf of bread on a cutting board, some bright orange jam, and a bowl of figs. She helped herself to all of it, even though figs were kind of hairy inside and tasted like practically nothing. Chewing a hard slice of the bread slathered with jam, she got madder and madder. It was one thing to flee sword-wielding Pazzis—whatever that was—and quite another to simply flee.

Maisie worked herself into such a fit of anger that she almost didn't see the note sticking out from beneath the wooden cutting board.

Well, she thought, feeling a teeny-tiny bit less mad, at least they left her a note.

She slid it out and stared at the writing on it. Immediately, Maisie recognized it as Leonardo's strange backward scrawling. But she didn't recognize even one word written there.

Frowning, Maisie tried to sound out the letters.

Ciao.

That was the only one she recognized because everyone knew *ciao* meant *good-bye.*

But shouldn't this *ciao* read as *good-bye?*

Up until this very instant, everything in Italian, or Tuscan, or Latin sounded like English to Maisie. And everything written in those languages appeared in English to her.

This note, however, was most definitely *not* in English. Maisie considered this.

Maybe it had something to do with the odd way that Leonardo wrote. His backward writing, all the letters jammed up close together, could possibly be just gibberish rather than any language at all.

Yes, she decided, this note was simply impossible to read.

Even though it probably had specific instructions on when and where to meet Felix and Leonardo, it was completely useless.

Like a lightbulb going off in a cartoon, an idea quickly came to Maisie.

Clutching the note, she ran to Leonardo's room. Inside, she went to the small mirror that hung above the table in one corner. The table had a ceramic pitcher sitting in a ceramic bowl on top of it, and a cotton towel draped across one corner. But it was the mirror that she needed.

Standing on tiptoe, Maisie lifted the note so that it was reflected there. That backward writing would appear forward now, she thought, congratulating herself on her brilliance.

Except even reflected in the mirror and reading it from left to right like regular writing, the words were still *not* in English.

There was *ciao* again. And her own name was legible now. And there were two signatures—*Felix* and *Leonardo*.

Everything else, Maisie saw, getting angry all over again, was in a language that was not English.

Confused, she balled the note up and stuck it in her pocket. Feeling how empty it was in there, she remembered dropping the seal into the urn last night. For the first time since she'd done that, she wondered if maybe that had been a bad idea. No, she decided as she made her way out of the bedroom and back to the studio, when the time came to go home she would just go back to the Palazzo Medici and retrieve it. Better to take one problem at a time, Maisie thought. For now, she would have to venture into the city and find Felix and Leonardo.

Felix glanced nervously around the crowd. From his special seat in the grandstand that held the Medicis and other nobility, he had a perfect view of everything—the Piazza Santa Croce below, the priests and dukes and other high-ranking officials of Florence around him, the bright, round colorful tents below that Leonardo had told him held the jousters, and the steaming crowd of what Sandro referred to—with a sneer—as *commoners*. Maisie was not anywhere to be seen.

Surely she had woken up by now and read the note telling her to come here to the Medici box. Why, Felix thought, did his sister have to be so difficult?

Felix sat between Piero and Leonardo. Although Piero seemed engaged in the goings-on below, Leonardo had one of his notebooks opened and had spent his time so far working on a sketch of a horse. He drew and studied what he drew and then, dissatisfied, rubbed off a line here and a line there, only to try again. Behind him, Sandro searched for a glimpse of someone named Simonetta. And beside Sandro sat Lorenzo's wife, Clarice. Other men from last night's supper were there, too, as well as women in damask and embroidered dresses.

But no Maisie.

"Morello di Vento has to win," Clarice said.

"Doesn't he always?" Sandro asked.

Leonardo leaned close to Felix and whispered, "That's Lorenzo's magnificent roan. He's won every race since Lorenzo took over from his father."

"The horses run from the Porta al Prato, through the Borgo Ognissanti, and end here," Piero explained. "That's why this is the most exciting place to be."

Horses began to near the Piazza Santa Croce.

Excited, everyone jumped to their feet.

Although most had riders in elaborate clothing, some horses were riderless. The riders wore spurs to goad the horses into running faster. By the time they reached the Piazza Santa Croce, the horses were in such a frenzy that some of them seemed to have gone mad. They foamed at the mouth and stood on their hind legs. Felix watched as several riders were thrown from their horses' backs.

But the first to ride triumphantly into the Piazza Santa Croce was indeed Lorenzo de' Medici.

When he appeared, his horse regal and swift, the crowd went wild with cheers and applause.

Except, Felix noticed, one group. The men there stared coldly down at Lorenzo as he waved from high on the back of his horse, victorious.

"The Pazzis," Leonardo said when he saw where Felix was looking. "They are rivals to the Medicis. Some say they are planning a take over."

"Are they?" Felix asked.

Leonardo shrugged. "It's possible," he said.

"Are they who stormed the palazzo last night?"

"I believe so," Leonardo said.

More horses raced into the Piazza Santa Croce now, and the roar from the crowd made any more talking impossible. Leonardo turned his attention to the spectacle below. And Felix tried to do the same. But really one question kept getting in his way: where in the world was Maisie?

When Maisie stepped out of Verrocchio's studio into the streets of Florence, the city seemed electric with excitement. Vendors crowded the cobblestone alleys and large piazzas, selling hot chestnuts, wine, and sweets. The air smelled of sugar and sweat and horses and horse poop and oil and Florence's own particular smell all at the same time. Somehow, Maisie liked this combination and she paused to inhale it, happy again that she'd hidden the seal back at the Palazzo Medici, essentially keeping herself and Felix here for as long as she liked.

Two women stood watching her, their faces filled with curiosity. They didn't have the strange dyed-yellow hair like Clarice did, or the pasty-white faces. Instead, their dark hair was pulled up under pointy hats, and their olive skin and large brown eyes made them appear friendly.

Maisie smiled as she approached them.

"Excuse me," she said, and the women glanced at each other, confused.

Maisie continued anyway.

"Do you know where the Medicis might be? I think Lorenzo is in some kind of race?"

At the name Medici, the women looked startled.

One of them said something to Maisie so rapidly that Maisie couldn't understand her.

"I'm sorry," Maisie said. "Where are they?"

Again, the women glanced at her, confused.

In the distance, the sound of a crowd cheering and thundering horses' hooves could be heard.

The other woman pointed in the direction of the noise and said something else unintelligible.

"That way?" Maisie asked. "The Medicis?"

The name Medici had the same effect on the women, who nodded and stepped away from Maisie, letting themselves get swallowed up by the growing crowd.

What in the world is wrong with them? Maisie wondered as she headed in the direction they'd indicated.

But it was difficult to follow sounds, and soon Maisie realized she'd walked in a circle, the cheers growing at first nearer and then, after several wrong turns, distant again.

This time Maisie approached a group of five boys about her age. They stood munching some kind of fried sweets from paper cones, and pushing and elbowing each other in the way boys at home did, too.

"Hi," Maisie said.

"Hi," the tallest, most handsome boy repeated,

sending the others into a fit of laughter.

"Hi," another one said.

"Hi," the other three echoed.

"O . . . kay," Maisie said, wondering why boys everywhere, even in Italy, even hundreds of years ago, acted exactly the same way. "I'm looking for the, I don't know, Medici seats? Or maybe they have, like, a box somewhere? Lorenzo is in a horse race?"

At first, the boys just stared at her, their mouths gaping open.

Then the tall one—the leader, Maisie realized—said, "*Non capisco*."

"*Non capisco*," Maisie repeated. "Is that near the Palazzo or—"

"*Non capisco*," the boy said again, more adamantly.

"*Non capisco*, I got it. But I'm not from here, so I'm not sure where exactly that is."

The boy laughed, throwing his arms up in defeat.

They all joined him, laughing and talking all at once. Maisie couldn't really make out what they were saying, though she heard the name Medici and something like Piazza Santa Croce.

"Thanks for nothing," she muttered angrily as she walked away.

Once again she tried to follow the sounds of the distant crowds. She stopped periodically to ask directions from people who seemed kind or helpful.

"*Non capisco?*" she asked one after the other. "This way?"

But each time they looked back at her puzzled or amused or disinterested.

After a very long time, Maisie finally glimpsed what had to be this *non capisco* place. She saw horses and men with long swords, more vendors, men and women dressed in finery, jesters, and musicians.

Relieved, Maisie made her slow way through the revelers.

Now all she had to do was find Felix.

Lorenzo joined Felix and the others, his face awash with the excitement of his victory.

"Time for the jousting," he said as he took his seat between Clarice and his brother, Giuliano.

As if they had been waiting for Lorenzo to sit down, the jousters took their positions at opposite ends of the piazza, their faces completely covered with shiny silver helmets, lances held high. One horse wore red-and-white stripes, the other black with elaborate gold trim. Their faces were covered, too, in intricate gold masks. A wooden barrier called a *tilt* separated the opponents. To prevent collisions, Piero had explained when Felix asked what that was. Leonardo had added that it also provided the best angle for breaking the lance.

Earlier, Leonardo had pointed out the Tree of Arms below, where colorful shields hung. The point of a joust, he'd explained, was not to kill or even hurt your opponent. To Felix's great relief, Leonardo said that if a rider or his horse was hit, the combatant would be disqualified. Instead, they tried for a hit right at the center of the shield, or to knock their opponent off his horse to score points. "Can you imagine how difficult it is to stay on your horse in one hundred pounds of armor holding that heavy lance?" Leonardo had speculated.

The crowd went wild with excitement, their shouts sending a shiver through Felix. For a moment, he let himself stop worrying about Maisie and gave over to the thrill of being here in Florence during the Renaissance watching a jousting tournament with Leonardo da Vinci and Piero della Francesca.

He wasn't going to let Maisie ruin this day for

him. Soon enough, they would give Leonardo that seal, and no doubt he would give them a lesson, and Felix would find himself back home in Newport. For right now at least, Felix was going to enjoy this jousting tournament. And if Maisie still hadn't shown up here when it was over—even though they'd left her a note with very specific directions— he was going to enjoy the rest of this day.

CHAPTER 11

THE SHARD

Maisie stood at the edge of the piazza, which had been turned into an arena surrounded by colorful tents. Shields with fancy coats of arms hung from a large tree, and hundreds—maybe thousands—of people sat on benches arranged auditorium-style around the arena. She was so busy scanning the faces in the crowd that Maisie didn't realize that she was wandering right into the arena itself. And she didn't see the two jousters positioned at opposite ends on their fancily bedecked horses, lances held high.

An announcement was made, sending the crowd into an uproar.

Still, Maisie didn't pause.

Felix and the others *had* to be up there somewhere!

Maisie, face turned upward toward the crowd, walked backward directly into the center of the arena, just as the jousters thundered toward each other.

People were shouting, but Maisie couldn't understand that they were yelling *Stop! Stop!*

The knights, their silver helmets lowered, could only hear the usual muffled sounds.

The knight on the horse in red and white had a clear shot at his opponent's shield. He aimed his lance, his horse speeding forward, a cloud of dust and red dirt kicked up behind them.

The sound of the horse's hooves pounding behind her made Maisie stop and turn.

Her eyes grew wide with fright and her mouth dropped open, a scream catching in her throat.

That knight was coming right for her!

The lance glistened in the sunlight, high above her.

She began to run, only to find a second horse and jouster racing toward her from the opposite direction.

A wall ran the length of the arena between the two jousters, but it was too high for Maisie to climb.

She looked over her shoulder again.

The jouster was almost right upon her!

At the perfect moment, the knight thrust his

lance at his opponent's shield, and jabbed hard.

At the exact same moment, Maisie ducked.

The crowd was on its feet, screaming.

Maisie felt something powerful hit her in the back, and then she was lifted off the ground, the roar of the crowd deafening now.

The other jouster raced past as Maisie seemed to fly above the wall and the arena itself.

Suddenly the crowd's yells turned into raucous laughter.

Maisie stopped moving, her arms and legs dangling in the air.

Slowly, she looked behind her to find the jouster's helmet lifted and his angry face glaring at her.

Her gaze drifted from his face to his arm, which was outstretched, his lance still in the air.

And at the end of that lance hung Maisie herself, midair.

Luckily, instead of stabbing *her*, the lance grabbed her by the shirt, piercing it.

The knight was saying something to her in his angry voice, but either fear or the crowd's laughter made it impossible for her to understand him.

Slowly, he lowered the lance and Maisie to the

ground, and slid the point from her shirt.

In the Medici grandstand, Leonardo looked at Felix.

"Isn't that your sister?" he asked.

Felix groaned. Of course it was his sister. Only Maisie would run between two jousters like that.

"I'll go get her," Felix said unhappily.

As he stood to leave, Sandro grinned at him.

"Better keep her away from that jouster," he said. "He was certain he was going to win. But because he hit your sister, he lost the joust."

"Great," Felix muttered as he hurried down the grandstand.

"I don't know why you're so mad at *me*," Maisie said. "You're the one who left without me."

"Didn't you read the note?" Felix said, stomping back toward the grandstand. "We gave you very specific directions on how to get here and where we'd be sitting."

"It looked like gibberish," Maisie said, equally as angry. "Have you ever tried to read Leonardo's handwriting? It's impossible!"

"Just stick by my side, will you?" Felix said.

She wanted to remind him how last night he was the one who took off with Leonardo, leaving her alone during the raid. But he was already sliding into a row of seats. Maisie saw Sandro grinning at her, and Lorenzo glaring at her, and Clarice giggling behind a gold-and-black fan, and a sea of other faces all looking directly at her.

"Sorry," Maisie said, even though she wasn't at all sorry.

She could have been killed! Stabbed by that giant lance!

Sandro, still grinning, said something to her that sounded like *Tootsie Pops*.

"They have Tootsie Pops here?" Maisie said, confused.

Felix rolled his eyes.

"Tootsie Pops? What is wrong with you?" he demanded.

"What's wrong with *me*?" Maisie demanded back at him.

"He said you're crazy, and I agree," Felix said.

Maisie frowned.

Now Lorenzo was talking to her, and by his tone she could tell he was chiding her. But the words coming out of his mouth made no sense at all.

Leonardo leaned closer to Maisie. "*Non capisco?*" he said.

"Not that again!" Maisie exclaimed. "What exactly is this *capisco* place?"

Leonardo was studying her face so closely that Maisie told him to get away. But he didn't move. Instead he turned toward Felix and started talking in . . .

Wait a minute, Maisie thought.

Leonardo was speaking in Italian.

And so were Lorenzo and Sandro.

Maisie's hand jumped to her neck where the shard hung from its piece of yarn.

All she felt there was her own skin, and the two tiny scabs that had formed on her neck from the sword grazing her last night.

Her fingers moved at first slowly, feeling for the shard, and then frantically as she realized that the shard was missing.

"Felix?" Masie said.

"What now?" he asked, peeved.

She pointed to her neck.

"Big deal," he said. "You've got a little cut or

something there. Honestly, Maisie, you need to—"

"The shard," she said.

Felix threw his arms over his head in frustration. "What about it, Maisie?"

"It's gone," she said.

"How could you lose the shard?" Felix shrieked as soon as they had left the Medici box and were making their way out of the arena.

"I don't know," Maisie said. "I didn't even realize it was gone until just now."

"The only way we're going to find it is if you can remember when you last saw it."

"That's ridiculous," Maisie said. "When's the last time you saw yours?"

"I touch the thing a million times a day," Felix said, frustrated. "Do you know why?"

He didn't wait for her to reply.

"I'll tell you why! Because I want to be sure it's still there!"

"Good for you," Maisie said. "Mr. Perfect. Mr. Does Everything Right."

"Did you understand what people were saying when you were on your way here?" Felix demanded.

"Because if you can remember that, at least we have a chance to find it by retracing your steps."

"Yes," Maisie said, insulted. "I asked a bunch of people where the Medicis were. And they all told me *non capisco*."

"*Non capisco*?" Felix repeated. "What's that?"

By now they had made their way back to the streets and they stood facing each other, both of them angry.

"This is *non capisco*," Maisie said, gesturing back toward the arena.

"No, it's not," Felix said. "This is the Piazza Santa Croce."

"Says who?" Maisie asked, trying to sound confident.

"Says everybody!" Felix said. "Because that's what it is!"

Maisie considered this.

"Then I guess I lost the shard back at Verrocchio's studio," she finally said. "I guess when I asked people where to go, they were telling me something I couldn't understand."

"At least that's a start," Felix said, heading off in that direction without even waiting for Maisie.

"But what if I lost it on the street between the studio and wherever I first asked someone for directions?" Maisie said when she caught up.

"Well, then we're in trouble, I guess." Felix said.

The shard was not in Verrocchio's studio.

Maisie and Felix looked everywhere: They shook her blankets out; they crawled along the floors, swiping their hands along them as they did; they lifted the wooden cutting board; they looked inside the jar of jam; they lifted every piece of paper and every paintbrush and every jar of paint and everything else on every surface in the studio; they looked behind canvases; they looked in corners; they even looked in rooms where Maisie had not gone.

No shard.

Exhausted and frustrated, Maisie and Felix stood, empty-handed.

"Whatever are you two looking for?" came a female voice.

They turned to find Clarice de' Medici standing watching them.

Of course, Felix understood exactly what she said. But Maisie did not. To her, it sounded like gibberish.

She sighed.

"Um . . . ," Felix said. "Maisie lost . . . her necklace."

Clarice frowned.

"What kind of necklace?"

"Just a small piece of porcelain on a thread," Felix said. Then he added, "It had sentimental value."

"What are you doing here, anyway?" Maisie asked, forgetting that Clarice couldn't understand her, either.

"What?" Clarice said, confused.

"Could you please not say anything?" Felix said to Maisie. "For once?"

"Fine," Maisie muttered.

He was right, of course. But she didn't want to admit that.

"Did you follow us here?" Felix asked Clarice.

She blushed.

"Well, yes," she said.

"Why?"

"I can't explain it," she said thoughtfully. "You two seem like you're from somewhere far away."

"We are," Felix said quickly.

"And the astrologer said—" Clarice stopped abruptly.

"What did he say?"

Her blush deepened. "Well, he said you were performing magic of some kind. Maybe even black magic."

Felix forced a laugh. "Magic? Us?"

Clarice didn't laugh. She just waited.

"What's she saying?" Maisie whispered.

Felix shot her a look to be quiet.

"I guess when people come from different places, they look so unusual that some people don't trust them," Felix offered.

"I suppose," Clarice said slowly, considering this.

"For example, where we come from, women don't dye their hair like you. At least, most women don't. And they don't pluck away all their hair here," he added, touching his forehead.

"Really?" Clarice said, interested.

"And they also don't put all that white stuff on their face."

"But light skin is beautiful," Clarice said. She glanced at Maisie. "I suppose if you're born with it, you wouldn't have to use face powder," she said.

"We have very different ideas of what's beautiful," Felix said.

"Hmmm," Clarice answered.

"We dress differently and—"

"What is the place called that you come from?" Clarice asked, surprising him so much that Felix answered honestly.

"The United States of America."

"I've never heard of it," Clarice said, doubt crossing her face.

Of course you haven't, Felix thought. *It hasn't been discovered yet.*

Maisie was staring at him in disbelief.

"Did you just tell her we were from the United States?" she said.

"Shhh," Felix ordered.

"Where is it?" Clarice was asking. "Near France? Or England?"

Felix shook his head.

"Much farther than that," he said. "It's across a big ocean."

"But if you went across the ocean," Clarice said, "you'd fall off the edge of the earth."

"What? No," Felix said.

"Yes," Clarice said. "Everyone knows that. The world is flat, and if you go too far, you fall off."

"The world isn't flat," Felix said. "It's round."

Clarice laughed.

"Either you're teasing me or you're crazy," she said.

A vague thought came into Felix's mind. Didn't they kill people who they thought were witches? Didn't they kill people who challenged what they believed to be true?

He forced a smile. "Of course I'm teasing you," he said. "How silly! The world, round!"

She laughed, relieved.

"Are you from somewhere near India?" she asked.

Felix took a long hard look at Clarice.

"Yes," he said. "Right near India."

"Things are very different there," Clarice said.

Felix nodded.

"How come you're so quiet, Maisie?" Clarice asked, startling Maisie.

Before his sister could say anything, Felix said, "She has a sore throat."

He pointed to Maisie's neck and gave a little cough.

Clarice's eyes widened.

"Did that happen last night when the Pazzis burst in?" she asked softly, one slender finger touching the two small dots on Maisie's neck.

"Yes," Felix said.

"That explains it," Clarice said.

"Explains . . . ?"

"This," Clarice said, and she opened a small purse around her waist and pulled out a long piece of thread.

Maisie grinned.

The shard hung from the center.

"Maisie's necklace," Felix said gratefully.

Clarice handed it to Maisie.

"I guess when that sword grazed her, it cut the thread," Clarice said. "The maid found this under the table this morning."

Maisie grinned even more.

She was holding the shard. And she understood everything that Clarice had just said.

CHAPTER 12

CARNIVAL!

The next day, Maisie and Felix were invited to walk in the Grand Procession. They would wear their masks and costumes—a black hat and coat for Felix, a long red velvet dress with lacing across the bodice for Maisie. Felix, of course, didn't like his costume. At all.

"It's scary!" he protested when he and Maisie went to retrieve the masks and clothes at Sandro's studio. "You know I don't like scary costumes."

Maisie sighed in frustration.

"I don't understand you, Felix," she said. "A great Renaissance artist makes you a mask, and you're complaining because it's too scary."

"It's the *Plague* Doctor!" Felix said, exasperated.

"But it's great," Maisie insisted. "When will you ever get a costume like this again?"

"Well, I don't understand *you*," Felix said, putting the coat and hat on, the mask tucked under one arm.

"Fine," Maisie said.

"Fine," Felix said.

The streets were so crowded that it was hard for Maisie and Felix to stay together. People pushed between them and behind them, and more than once Felix lost sight of Maisie. Her blond hair made it easy for him to spot her, but as the crowd thickened it became more and more difficult.

This time, even on tiptoe he couldn't find her.

"Maisie!" Felix called, to no avail. The sounds of the crowd combined with music and the clopping of horses' hooves drowned out his voice.

He was walking along the Arno, still on tiptoe, when a strong hand clasped his shoulder, halting him.

Felix glanced back and up into the face of a red-robed priest scowling at him.

"It's almost time for the *vergognosi* to begin," the priest said, yanking Felix from the crowd.

Priests have a lot of power here, Felix thought as the crowd separated for them.

The priest kept a firm hand on Felix as he maneuvered through the streets. With a sinking feeling, Felix realized he and Maisie were getting separated again. At least this time they knew to meet Leonardo at the start of the procession.

"You weren't even heading toward the Piazza degli Innocenti, were you?" the priest said when they reached a piazza.

"No," Felix said, "actually my sister and I—"

Boom!

The priest slapped Felix on the side of the head.

"Don't be impertinent!" he barked.

"Ouch!" Felix said, rubbing his head, which earned him another slap.

"Now join the others," the priest said, giving Felix a shove.

The others appeared to be . . . boys. More boys than Felix had ever seen in one place, all of them lined up beneath flags, their hands joined together.

One of the boys made room for Felix to join them.

What else could he do?

Slowly, Felix took the spot the boy offered, taking the clammy hand of one boy and the rough hand of another.

They all faced a church with a statue of a saint or something in front of it.

The clammy-hand boy whispered, awed, "Our Lady of the Annunziata."

The priest mumbled some prayers.

The boys repeated whatever he said.

A trumpet sounded, and as if that was their cue, all the boys got in formation and began to march.

They marched out of the piazza to the Arno River, crowds following them as they moved.

Felix tried to do exactly what the others did so as not to get another slap on the head. Still, he fell behind as he searched in vain for Maisie and had to scurry to catch up.

Finally, they arrived at San Marco cathedral.

Trumpets announced their arrival, and people threw flowers in their path. For an instant, Felix felt special, even though he had no idea why these boys were doing this, or why everyone had come out to see them.

Inside the packed cathedral, people reached out

and began to give the boys things: silverware, veils, and coins. At first, Felix said, "No, thank you," when someone tried to thrust something into his hands, but eventually, afraid to stand out, he, too, accepted their gifts.

The coins would at least come in handy, he decided as he jammed them into his pockets. One of the problems with time traveling was never having any money. Now he and Maisie would be able to buy food if they got hungry. But he had no idea what he would do with the enormous silver candlestick or the elegantly carved spoons.

A voice cut through the racket.

"Felix?"

Felix turned toward it, and there stood Leonardo looking as puzzled as Felix felt.

When Leonardo stepped from the crowd to rescue Felix, a murmur spread through the cathedral. Already, Leonardo was considered an artist to pay attention to, someone whom the Medicis had taken under their wing. Even the priest allowed him to escort Felix from the group of boys and lead him out of the cathedral.

"Do you need that candlestick?" Leonardo teased.

"Uh, no," Felix said, setting it down on the steps of San Marco.

"I see the cardinal thought you were one of the *vergognosi,*" Leonardo said as they walked through the cobblestone streets.

"That's what he said!"

"Children collecting for the poor," Leonardo explained, steering Felix down one alley and then quickly down another. "A few years ago these boys stood on the street corners throwing stones at the Carnival revelers. So this is an improvement."

They had reached the piazza where everyone was meeting for the procession. There, at the edge of the crowd, stood Maisie and Sandro. In her red velvet dress and white-and-gold mask, her curls spilling down, Maisie looked so beautiful that Felix almost forgot how angry he was at her.

He opened his mouth to call to her, but Leonardo pulled him away.

"Before we join the others," Leonardo said seriously, "I want to talk with you."

"Okay," Felix said, trying to keep an eye on Maisie before she vanished again.

"About the future," Leonardo said. "About going there with you."

"I would take you if I could," Felix said. "But it doesn't work that way."

Leonardo nodded enthusiastically.

"Exactly," he said. "If I must stay here, then please tell me how it *does* work. What makes it possible? How do you get here? How do you get back?"

"I don't really know," Felix admitted. "Maisie and I touch an object that our great-great-grandfather collected a hundred years ago, and we start to lift off the ground—"

"Wait!" Leonardo said.

He took one of his notebooks from a pocket and began to scribble in it.

"Then what?" he asked.

"Well, it's hard to explain. But we kind of tumble . . . you know . . . do somersaults, and everything is black all around us. It's windy, and the wind smells . . . it smells wonderful. Like all of our favorite things."

Leonardo's brow furrowed with concentration.

"And then, without warning, it all stops."

Leonardo looked up from his notebook.

"It stops and—?"

"And for a second . . . no, less than a second . . . we are suspended, kind of."

Felix paused.

"It's hard to describe," he said finally.

"Is it thrilling?"

Felix shook his head. "It's scary. I don't know, maybe Maisie thinks it's thrilling."

"And then what?"

"Then we drop and land, hard. In the ocean or in a barn or, well, in your studio."

Leonardo looked wistful. "And then you have traveled backward in time."

Felix nodded.

Leonardo didn't say anything for what seemed a long while. Behind them, musicians had begun to play, and music filled the air.

"In rivers," Leonardo said thoughtfully, "the water that you touch is the last of what has passed and the first of that which comes. So it is with present time. I suppose I must be satisfied with this."

Back when Maisie and Felix were little, their parents used to take them to the Macy's Thanksgiving

Day Parade. Maisie could remember getting up early on Thanksgiving morning, her father standing at the stove making Mexican hot chocolate for them, which was super rich and spicy. Her mother made the homemade whipped cream to put on top, adding just the right amount of vanilla as she whipped it. They'd have croissants from the French bakery down the street that her father had gone to get as soon as the bakery opened so that they were still a little warm by the time they sat down to eat. Felix and their mother liked the plain ones; but Maisie and her father liked almond.

Then, with the streets of their neighborhood still asleep, they walked the twenty blocks to find a good spot to watch the parade. Maisie could still remember how it felt to sit on her father's shoulders as the first float rounded the corner. If she closed her eyes, she could almost feel her fingers in his curly hair, feel the cold November air.

Those memories wrapped themselves around her now as the first float entered the piazza.

"I love this," she said softly, to no one in particular.

But Sandro heard her and smiled.

"Let's join the procession now, shall we?"

Maisie hesitated. She should wait for Felix, but once again he had gone off somewhere with Leonardo, even though they'd agreed to meet here. She didn't understand him at all.

"Yes," Maisie said firmly. "Let's."

They walked along the edge of the piazza to the point where they could enter the parade.

"Hello, Sandro," a woman's voice said.

Sandro halted.

"Simonetta," he said in a hushed voice.

Maisie immediately recognized the name. Here was the woman whose window they had stood under the other night, Sandro hoping for a glimpse of her. Although it was hard to tell what she looked like beneath the silver-and-feathered mask she wore, Maisie saw Simonetta's long blond hair and smooth alabaster skin.

"Happy Carnival," Simonetta said, brushing close past Sandro as she hurried off.

Sandro stood, frozen in place, watching her.

"Come on," Maisie said, tugging his sleeve.

With a sad sigh, he slowly moved forward again.

But he quickly looked less distracted as they were swept into the joyous procession, lost among the musicians, jesters, fellow participants, and floats, all moving out of the piazza and into the streets of Florence.

At last, Felix and Leonardo also joined the procession. Of course Maisie hadn't waited for him. *Again*, Felix thought in frustration. But he didn't want his sister to ruin the day, so he accepted the noisemaker someone thrust in his hand and shook up and down, adding to the cacophony.

Like a giant serpent, the procession snaked through the narrow streets until it reached the Arno River. There, it followed the curve of the river. Voices from a float covered in fresh lilies—the flower of Florence, Leonardo explained—called out to Leonardo and Felix.

"Join us!"

Leonardo grinned. "There's your sister and Sandro Botticelli."

Felix was about to protest, but Leonardo left the line to race toward them. Felix followed, reluctantly.

But once on the float, able to look down at the procession and across the river to the rooftops and hills of Florence, he was happy he had come.

Maisie, however, was scowling at him.

"You never showed up!" she said.

"You left me!" he reminded her. "And a priest grabbed me and—"

"Why can't you just stick by my side?"

"Why can't you stick by *my* side?"

They glared at each other.

"I don't understand you anymore," they both said at almost the exact same time.

"Ah!" Leonardo told them. "That is a problem. You must try harder to listen to each other. To understand each other's point of view."

Maisie shot him an angry look. "You have no idea all the things we are supposed to understand that don't make sense. Why our parents aren't together. Why our mother is with a dope named Bruce Fishbaum. Why—"

"Maisie," Leonardo said, interrupting. "And Felix, too. The noblest pleasure is the joy of understanding."

Leonardo's words settled in Felix's mind.

The noblest pleasure is the joy of understanding.

Felix looked at Maisie, who was looking right back at him.

The noblest pleasure is the joy of understanding.

Leonardo had just given them the lesson they most needed to hear. But they were still on the float, the smell of lilies all around them, moving along the Arno River in Renaissance Florence.

"Why are we still here?" Felix whispered to her.

Maisie avoided his gaze.

"Maisie?"

"We haven't given him the seal," she muttered.

"That's right!" Felix said. "I think it's time, don't you?"

Maisie didn't answer.

"I don't have it," Felix reminded her.

Maisie turned toward him.

"Neither do I," she said.

CHAPTER 13

AMY PICKWORTH'S MESSAGE

"You did what?" Felix gasped.

The procession had ended, and Maisie and Felix were heading with a large group to the Palazzo Medici for a banquet.

"It's no big deal," Maisie said. "I put it in one of those big urns. We'll get it as soon as we arrive."

"What if it's not there?"

"Why do you have to worry so much?" Maisie asked, rhetorically.

"Why can't you just do what you're supposed to do?"

"Maybe I didn't want to go back to Bruce Fishbaum, and Dad in a hotel, and everything upside down!" Maisie blurted.

"I don't understand why you can't accept . . ."

Felix stopped himself, Leonardo's words ringing in his ears.

He took a deep breath.

"I don't like Bruce Fishbaum much, either," he told Maisie. "But Mom does."

After all, Felix realized, they had to try to understand *her* as well.

"How can she?" Maisie said.

"It's an adult thing, I think," he admitted.

"I thought after Agatha called off the wedding that Mom would see the chance to reunite with Dad."

"I guess they don't want to get back together, Maisie. And I guess we have to understand that."

Tears sprang to Maisie's eyes.

"So you think they're divorced forever?" she asked.

"I do."

"Well," Maisie said, wiping the tears from her face with the back of her hand, "I don't have to like it."

Felix smiled at her. "No," he said. "You don't."

Together they walked through the front doors of the Palazzo Medici and into the courtyard.

The banquet table was practically drooping from

the platters of meat and pasta and vegetables, the jugs of wine, the cheeses and fruits.

But Maisie led Felix away from the table, across the courtyard toward the terra-cotta urn.

Abruptly, she stopped.

"What now?" he asked her.

"The urn was right over there," Maisie said, pointing to an empty corner.

"Oh no," Felix groaned.

Maisie's gaze flitted from one corner to the next until she'd determined that the urn was indeed gone.

Clarice appeared in front of them, a quizzical expression on her face.

"There's food, and soon Leonardo will sing a song he wrote especially for Carnival," she said.

"Thanks," Felix remembered to say, despite his growing anxiety. Without that urn, the seal was missing. And without that seal, they would never go back home to Newport and their parents.

"What's the matter?" Clarice asked them.

"Nothing," Maisie said quickly.

She forced a laugh. "You know," she continued, "the other night I thought there was this big urn over there."

She pointed to the empty corner.

"There was," Clarice said. "Those terrible Pazzis smashed it. Lorenzo has commissioned something even better, more beautiful. In fact, we'll have a sculpture in every corner!"

"They smashed it?" Felix said, his stomach sinking.

"To smithereens. It was unsalvageable. We had to throw every piece away," Clarice said. "And that was an antiquity. Irreplacable!" She added under her breath, "Those Pazzis!"

"How terrible," Maisie managed to say.

"Where did you say you threw those pieces?" Felix asked hopefully.

Clarice laughed. "I have no idea. The servants take care of things like that."

She studied their faces in that serious unnerving way she had.

"Why are you two so concerned with a broken urn, anyway?" she asked them.

"I just . . . um . . . admire antiquities," Maisie stammered.

"O-*kay*," Clarice said doubtfully.

Felix and Maisie looked at her as innocently as they could, holding her gaze until she finally said,

"Well, then, come and eat."

"Great," Felix said.

"Oh, by the way," Maisie said, trying to keep her voice light. "In all the excitement the other night, what with the Pazzis breaking everything and me hiding, I lost the seal I use on my letters."

Clarice's thin eyebrows arched.

"Really?"

"It's gold? With the *giglio* on it?" Maisie continued.

"Hmmm," Clarice said.

"I think I dropped it"—Maisie giggled—"in that urn."

"You dropped it in the urn?" Clarice repeated.

Leonardo had made his way over to the three of them, his lute beneath his arm.

"I'm about to play," he told them.

"One minute, Leonardo," Clarice said.

She motioned to one of the servants, who scurried over to them.

"Madame?" he said.

"Aren't you the one who took care of the urn the Pazzis destroyed?" she asked.

"Yes, madame."

"Was there anything in it?"

"Yes, madame," he said. "I gave it to Signor Medici."

"A gold seal?" Maisie blurted.

The servant looked at her sternly. "Yes, miss," he said.

"Great!" Maisie said happily. "I'll just get it from Lorenzo."

Leonardo grabbed Felix's arm.

"That's the object?" he asked. "When you give that to me, you'll return to the twenty-first century?"

"Yes," Felix said.

Leonardo nodded solemnly.

"I understand that you need to go back," he said.

"Understanding is the noblest joy," Felix said.

Lorenzo had *retired* to his chambers. That's what Clarice told Maisie when she went looking for him. And the seal.

"Um," Maisie said, "I kind of need to see him."

Clarice smiled, revealing her small and slightly crooked teeth. "When he is rested," she said.

"When will that be?" Maisie asked.

Clarice smiled again, and shrugged.

"And," Clarice added, "I think I need some rest,

too. What a marvelous day it's been!"

Maisie watched Clarice walk away, climbing the staircase to the family's private quarters.

Well, Maisie thought, *I'll just have to wake up Lorenzo.*

She gave Clarice time to get upstairs before she followed.

Maisie had not been up to the private quarters before, and the first thing she noticed was how much art they had. Paintings hung crowded together on every wall, leaving almost no blank space at all. Sculptures stood by doorways and in corners, some of them with arms broken off or pieces missing, others shiny white marble. She paused in front of two portraits, one of Lorenzo and one of Clarice, both of them dressed in formal clothes. She tried to imagine having to sit for a painter to get a portrait done. How did Clarice manage to do so many adult things, even though she was just a teenager? *There's a good reason to live in the twenty-first century,* Maisie decided as she continued down the long high-ceilinged hall.

Everywhere she looked she saw gold glittering back at her, or people in paintings staring at her. And doors. Closed doors to more rooms than Elm Medona had. Maisie had no choice. She stopped at each one and pushed it open carefully, just enough to peer inside. The first appeared to be a study filled with floor-to-ceiling books, and of course more sculptures and paintings. The next looked like a living room, all velvet furniture and giant tapestries covering the long stretch of walls. The tapestries were faded and showed scenes of what looked at a glance like rural life. Not the room she needed, so she quietly shut the door and continued past marble benches with mosaic scenes embedded in them, to still more doors that, when opened, revealed more studies and living rooms.

Finally, she glimpsed a room beyond one of the living rooms, and in that second room was a fireplace with a crackling fire burning and a narrow high bed covered in heavy red linens. The bed had four tall, intricately carved posts and a red canopy with fringe dangling from it. And in that bed lay Lorenzo the Magnificent.

Maisie stepped inside the first room, walking heavily to try to wake him and closing the door with a firm bang.

It worked.

Lorenzo sat upright and grabbed a large shiny knife from beside him.

"Put that down!" Maisie said. "It's only me, Maisie Robbins."

Lorenzo's face had gone pale, and color did not return immediately.

"What are you doing in my private chambers?" he said, his voice regal.

"I'm sorry," Maisie said. "But I think you have something of mine."

"Do you realize that I could have you thrown in prison? With the Pazzis' assassination threats, *anyone* who breaks in—"

"Actually," Maisie said, "I didn't break in. I was downstairs and—"

"Silence!" Lorenzo ordered.

How can a man in a red canopy bed, wearing a weird off-white nightgown, be so scary? Maisie wondered. Because Lorenzo, his cheeks now bright red, was indeed terrifying.

"Now I want you to turn around and leave my quarters."

"But—"

"Do you understand?" Lorenzo said, his dark eyes ablaze.

"I do," Maisie said, taking a few steps backward toward the door. "But I—"

"Prison is a very unpleasant place," Lorenzo said.

"Okay, okay," Maisie said. "But I need my gold seal back," she finished quickly as she rushed out the door.

Once back in the corridor, she leaned against a wall, trying to calm down. Behind her, she felt a picture go crooked. Maisie turned and straightened it, the saint with his gold halo and sad droopy eyes staring back at her.

"Miss Robbins," a deep voice called, startling her enough to make her send the painting back to a crooked angle.

A servant walked slowly toward her, holding a small yellow satin pillow.

"Yes?" Maisie asked, her voice little more than a squeak.

"Signor Medici believes this belongs to you."

There, sitting right in the middle of the pillow, the gold seal shone.

"Yes!" Maisie said with relief. "Yes!"

With that, Maisie returned, breathless, to the courtyard, waving the seal in the air.

Felix looked at Maisie. Leonardo did, too.

Leonardo put out his hand.

And Maisie placed the seal in his waiting palm.

The next morning, Maisie woke up to the sound of Great-Uncle Thorne's loud, boisterous voice echoing through the hall.

"Up! Up, you two rapscallions!" he shouted. "Awaken and greet the new day!"

Quieter, as if he were speaking to himself, he added, "I certainly have."

Maisie burst into a big grin. Great-Uncle Thorne was not at death's door, that terrible phrase her mother had used. He was alive! And he was here!

Quickly, she pulled on an old faded concert T-shirt of her father's and her fleece vest, slipped her feet into her sneakers, and without even bothering to tie the laces, ran out into the hall.

Her mother hovered behind Great-Uncle Thorne, mystified.

"I got a call from the hospital," she explained, "saying he woke up, then *got* up, and *then* demanded to come home right away."

"A miracle," Felix said from the doorway of his room, his eyes twinkling.

"Jennifer," Great-Uncle Thorne ordered, turning his gaze onto their mother, "tell Cook I would like an *omelette aux fines herbes*, a pot of *café au lait*, and some melon."

"All right," their mother said.

"*Tout de suite*," Great-Uncle Thorne added.

With that, their mother scurried off to the Kitchen.

As soon as she was gone, Great-Uncle Thorne turned his attention to Maisie and Felix.

"Let's go," he said to them.

"Go?" Maisie said. "Go where?"

He pointed a gnarled finger toward the door.

What choice did they have? Maisie and Felix let him lead the way out, down the stairs, and into the hallway, the wall closing behind them.

"Have you two ever been in the Fairy Room?" Great-Uncle Thorne asked them.

"Where's that?" Maisie asked.

"You'll see," he said.

They went down the Grand Staircase, across the foyer, through the West Rotunda with its glass-domed ceiling that revealed the full moon still in the sky above them, and into the Ladies' Drawing Room.

The Ladies' Drawing Room had pink moiré silk walls with twenty-four-carat-gold trim and a ceiling covered with murals of some Greek myth. Maisie and Felix hardly ever came in here. Everything was dainty and fragile-looking, from the desk with the spindly legs to the deep-pink fainting couch.

Great-Uncle Thorne paused.

"It's said that my mother loved this room," he said wistfully.

Maisie glanced around it. A harp stood in one corner with a music stand in front of it.

"Did you know that every harp has a twin, cut from the same piece of wood?" Great-Uncle Thorne asked them.

But it seemed to Felix to be a rhetorical question, so he didn't respond.

"Hey!" Maisie said, pointing to an oval painting on the south wall. "That's from the Palazzo Medici!"

"So it is," Great-Uncle Thorne said with a chuckle. "My sister would be pleased that you are finally learning some culture."

He moved slowly to the opposite wall.

On it were four large jewels.

"Are those real?" Maisie asked him.

Great-Uncle Thorne touched them in turn, saying what each was as he did.

"Emerald. Ruby. Sapphire. Diamond."

He kept his hand on the diamond and gently turned it until that part of the wall creaked open.

"It's a door!" Felix said.

"The door to the Fairy Room," Great-Uncle Thorne said, stepping inside.

Maise and Felix followed him, gasping as they entered.

The room was tiny, its walls covered with real ivy and pink and blue morning glories. The ceiling was covered in angel hair dotted with tiny twinkling white lights.

"The floor is made of grass!" Maisie exclaimed.

All of the furniture—which wasn't very much—glittered with gold.

There was a small love seat, and on that love seat sat the Ziff twins.

Rayne and Hadley jumped to their feet as soon as they saw Maisie and Felix.

"Isn't this room the most wonderful place you've

ever seen?" Rayne said, giddy.

"My mother built this for the fairies," Great-Uncle Thorne explained.

"Fairies," Maisie said.

"Yes," Great-Uncle Thorne explained. "In Victorian times, people—including my mother—were fascinated with fairies and their lore. Some—also perhaps including my mother—claimed to see them. She built this room for them, putting all of their favorite things in it."

"So they just flap their wings and fly in and out of here?" Maisie said sarcastically.

"Actually," Great-Uncle Thorne said, "fairies don't have wings. They fly by magic. That is, if you believe in that sort of thing. As I said, many people in the Victorian era did."

"Is that why we're all here?" Felix asked.

"Not at all," Great-Uncle Thorne said. "I just wanted the most private place for us to meet and finally let the Ziff twins, here, tell us what happened when they found Amy Pickworth."

Hadley began to talk right away.

"We saw her that very next day. She had on real bush gear. You know, khaki pants and a jacket with all these pockets and a big hat with, like, a veil over her face."

"To keep out the mosquitoes," Rayne explained.

"As we approached, she looked up from her work—"

"She was very engrossed in it, drawing a map of some kind—"

"—and she said, simply, 'You've come.'"

"We didn't know what to answer," Rayne said.

"She did ask us what year we'd come from—"

"—and when we told her, she got so excited!"

"She couldn't believe it was the twenty-first century," Hadley added.

"She asked about her children, and about Phinneas, and about history, too," Rayne said, her words spilling out rapidly.

"Who was president and what had happened in a lot of countries and with a lot of people I'd never heard of," Hadley continued.

"And then she said, 'It's time.'"

Maisie frowned. "It's time? That was her message?"

Rayne shook her head. "No. I asked her, 'Time for what?'"

"And she said," Hadley finished, "'Why, time to open the egg.'"

"The missing egg!" Felix said.

"She took the map we had, the one from The Treasure Chest, and then we were back," Rayne explained.

Maisie and Felix looked at Great-Uncle Thorne.

He stood tall, not at all bent or crooked, his eyes gleaming.

"Children," he said, "it's time to open the egg."

LEONARDO DA VINCI

Born: April 15, 1452

Died: May 2, 1519

Leonardo da Vinci was born in the town of Vinci in the Republic of Florence, which is now part of the country of Italy. At the time, Italy was not united and was made up of many city-states, or republics. It was customary for people to take the name of their birth city, which is why Leonardo was known as da Vinci—Leonardo from Vinci. Little is known of Leonardo's early life. His parents never married because they were from different economic and social classes. His mother was a peasant, possibly even a servant (though no one knows for sure). His father was a notary, which was similar to a lawyer. Leonardo lived with his mother until he was five and then moved to his father's family farm. Eventually, both of his parents married other people and had other children, giving Leonardo seventeen half brothers and sisters!

Leonardo did not have a formal education. But he began to draw the Tuscan landscape as well as the natural world around him on the farm at a very early age. He loved to read, and his grandfather taught him math and science. Through his love of observation, he taught himself astronomy, anatomy, and physics.

In 1468, Leonardo's family moved to Florence. At that time—now called the Renaissance—art was flourishing there. Leonardo's father helped get him an apprenticeship with Andrea del Verrocchio, a painter, sculptor, and goldsmith who took many apprentices, including Sandro Botticelli. Artists were valued in Renaissance Florence, and the wealthy people there became their patrons, securing commissions for them and welcoming them into their homes.

An artist's apprenticeship followed a rigorous program. In addition to studying the fundamentals of painting, he studied color theory, sculpting, and metalwork. Leonardo studied with Verrocchio until 1472, when he was admitted to Florence's painters' guild. This gave him credibility and visibility to wealthy patrons. After five years with the guild, Leonardo opened his own studio, where he worked mostly with oil paints. At that time in Florence, the Medicis were the most important political family, and Lorenzo de' Medici became Leonardo's patron (he was also Michelangelo's and Botticelli's patron). However, Leonardo had a habit of not finishing work he'd begun, and soon Lorenzo ended his patronage.

In 1482, Lorenzo went under the patronage of Ludovico Sforza, the future Duke of Milan. The Sforzas controlled Milan, but unlike the Medicis, who were bankers, the Sforzas were warriors, and Leonardo learned about machinery and military equipment in Milan. He served as the duke's chief military engineer and architect, but he also began *The Last Supper*, one of his most famous paintings, during this time. The duke commissioned it to be painted on the wall of the family chapel, which was thirty feet long by fourteen feet high. Due to the type of paint Leonardo used and the humidity in the chapel, the painting is extremely fragile and began to deteriorate almost immediately. In 1999, a restoration was completed, but very little of the original paint remains, and the expressions of the Apostles are difficult to make out.

In 1499, the duke was forced out of Milan, and King Louis XII of France took over all of his land. With the military experience Leonardo had gained with Sforza, he was able to get work with Cesare Borgia's army in 1502. Borgia was a notorious figure during the Renaissance. He allegedly killed his own brother, and many believe that Machiavelli based his book *The Prince* on Borgia. Although Borgia commissioned Leonardo to design bridges, catapults, cannons, and other weapons, he was also a patron of the arts, so Leonardo worked with him until 1503, when King Louis's governor made Leonardo the court painter in Milan.

Under King Louis, Leonardo continued to do military and architectural engineering in addition to painting. But he was also able to continue his studies in anatomy, botany, hydraulics, and other sciences. In 1513, King Louis XII was forced out of Milan, thus ending Leonardo's role in his court and freeing him to return to the Medici patronage. By this time, Lorenzo's son Giovanni had become pope (known as Pope Leo X), and another son, Giuliano, served as the head of the pope's army. As a result, Leonardo moved to Rome, where he had his own workshop and lived in the Vatican.

During his career, Leonardo developed a technique in painting called *sfumato*, a word that comes from the Italian sfumere, which means "to tone down" or "to evaporate like smoke." *Sfumato* is a fine shading that produces soft, almost invisible transitions between colors and tones using subtle gradations, without lines or borders, from light to dark areas. In Rome, Leonardo painted *St. John the Baptist*, which is considered the best example of *sfumato*.

For the last three years of his life, Leonardo worked in the court of Francois I, who became the king of France after Louis XII. Francois invited Leonardo to visit, and made him premier architect, engineer, and painter of his court. He was given a fine home near the palace in the Loire Valley and had no expectations placed on him but to be the king's friend. Leonardo spent his final years sketching and continuing his scientific studies and designs. In fact, his paintings of water moving and of whirlpools were used in scientific research of turbulence.

Leonardo's favorite of his own work was his most famous painting, the *Mona Lisa*. Completed in 1506, it is the smallest of his paintings—only thirty inches by twenty-one inches—and is oil painted on wood. Lisa Gherardini del Giocondo, Leonardo's neighbor, is believed to be the model for the *Mona Lisa*, though no one is 100 percent certain. The painting is famous for many reasons: it is an excellent example of *sfumato* and of *chiaroscuro* (a contrasting of light and shadow), but it is her expression that is most discussed about the painting. In it, her slight smile seems both innocent and knowing at the same time, and her eyes seem to follow you. Leonardo kept the painting with him until his death, at which point it became the property of King Francois. Although it now hangs in the Louvre Museum in Paris, it has also been in Napoleon's possession, hidden to protect it during the Franco-Prussian War and World War II, traveled to other countries and other museums, and was even stolen in 1911 by an Italian employee of the Louvre who believed it should reside in Italy. It was returned two years later. In 1956, part of the painting was damaged when a vandal threw acid at it, and later that same year, a rock was thrown at it, resulting in the loss of a speck of pigment near the left elbow. It is now protected by bulletproof glass.

Sandro Botticelli
May 20, 1455–May 17, 1510

Sandro Botticelli was born in Florence and became an apprentice when he was fourteen years old. He also studied under Andrea del Verrocchio, as well as the engraver Antonio del Pollaiuolo and the master painter Fra Filippo Lippi. Botticelli got his own workshop when he was twenty-five and stayed in Florence under the patronage of the Medicis and other wealthy families there. His most famous painting is *The Birth of Venus*, which he completed around 1486, and now hangs in the Uffizi Gallery in Florence. It is widely agreed that his model for Venus and other women in his work was Simonetta Vespucci, for whom he had an unrequited love. Simonetta died in 1476. The unmarried Botticelli asked that when he died, he be buried at her feet. His wish was carried out when he died thirty-four years later, and they are both buried in the Church of Ognissanti in Florence.

Piero della Francesca
Circa 1415–October 12, 1492

Although Piero della Francesca became one of the most admired painters of the Italian Renaissance, very little is known about his early life or his training as an artist. He was born in the Tuscan town of Borgo Santo Sepolcro sometime around 1415. Early records indicate that he may have apprenticed with a local painter before moving to Florence around 1439 to paint frescoes for a church there. In addition to art, he was also known as a brilliant mathematician.

Throughout his life, della Francesca received commissions to paint frescoes and altarpieces in churches in Tuscany and beyond. Though many of these have been lost or destroyed, his cycle of frescoes in the basilica of San Francesco in Arezzo is considered to be not only one of his masterpieces but also one of the masterpieces of the entire Renaissance. His painting *The Baptism of Christ* is probably the most representative of his style, in particular his use of color and light, which makes his paintings appear almost bleached.

Della Francesco never lost his ties with his small hometown, always returning there after time in cities. He spent the last two years of his life there. During that time, he is believed to have abandoned painting and returned to the study of mathematics and its relationship to painting. Interestingly, although he was respected by his peers, he did not have the influence many of them did. It wasn't until the twentieth century that he was recognized as a major artist of the Italian Renaissance.

I do so much research for each book in The Treasure Chest series and discover so many cool facts that I can't fit into every book. Here are some of my favorites from my research for *The Treasure Chest: #9 Leonardo da Vinci: Renaissance Master*. Enjoy!

One of my favorite cities in the whole world is Florence, Italy. I've been lucky enough to go there dozens of times and always find something new to see. The works of art of Leonardo da Vinci, Sandro Botticelli, and Michelangelo are all over the city, constant reminders of the lasting effects of the great art of the Renaissance.

In order to really appreciate the Renaissance, it's important to look back first at the Middle Ages and pre-Renaissance Italy. The Middle Ages, also called the Medieval Period or the Dark Ages, describes Europe between the fall of Rome in 476 CE and the beginning of the Renaissance in the fourteenth century. After the fall of the Roman Empire, no single state or government united the people, and the Catholic Church became so powerful that kings, queens, and other leaders derived *their* power from their alliances with the Church.

The influence of the Church's dominance during this period can be seen in many ways. In 1095, Pope Urban II authorized a holy army to fight nonbelievers all the way to Jerusalem. Known as the Crusades, this conflict continued for almost four hundred years. Another way to demonstrate devotion to the Church during this period was to build grand cathedrals. These cathedrals can still be visited in most of the cities throughout Europe.

In 1450, Johannes Gutenberg invented the first printing press; prior to that, many books were works of art handmade with gold and silver in monasteries and universities. These books were called illuminated manuscripts.

The political system during the Middle Ages was called feudalism. Peasants—also known as serfs—did the work on the large pieces of land that kings granted to noblemen. Most of the crops they planted and harvested went to the wealthy landowners. They also had to tithe—give 10 percent of their income to the church. In exchange for their labor, they were allowed to live free on the land and to get protection from the king.

Agricultural innovations such as the heavy plow and three-field crop rotation in the eleventh century made farming more efficient. As a result, fewer farm workers were needed. People began to move into the cities. Because of the Crusades, goods from distant lands were in demand, and ports were developed to receive these goods. Some European cities reached populations of fifty thousand citizens by 1300.

The unification of Italy did not happen for many centuries. During the pre-Renaissance, it was made up of city-states that always battled with each other. As Italy moved toward the Renaissance, a word which means *rebirth*, artists—many of them in Florence—helped shape the transition from the feudalistic Middle Ages to this new age of enlightenment.

The architect Filippo Brunelleschi combined elements of classical architecture with newer ideas in structures such as the Duomo of the cathedral of Santa Maria del Fiore in Florence. The architect Leon Battista Alberti was one of the first to include the use of perspective in his designs, which he combined with classicism in such buildings as Santa Maria Novello in Florence. Also during this pre-Renaissance time,

Dante wrote *The Divine Comedy*, and Giotto, credited with breathing life back into painting, popularized and revived art.

It is widely acknowledged that the Renaissance began in Florence, where bankers, merchants, and other wealthy members of society began to support the arts. The Medicis were the richest family in Italy—perhaps in all of Europe. Under Cosimo de' Medici, and then Lorenzo the Magnificent, artists were commissioned to paint, sculpt, and build private and public works of art. In medieval times, the Church sponsored art. But now wealthy families employed artists for the duration of a work of art's completion (which was often years), as well as supplying room and board and access to other wealthy families. This was a system that nurtured artists.

There is no precise date when the Renaissance came to an end, and there is no agreed upon reason for it. Many point to France's invasion of Italy as the beginning of the end. Others point to the rise of power of the monk Savonarola and his subsequent brief rule, during which many works of art were destroyed in what was known as the "Bonfire of the Vanities" in the center of Florence. A few years later a wide array of

Renaissance works of literature were banned.

Just as important was the end of stability with a series of foreign invasions known as the Italian Wars beginning in 1494 when France wreaked widespread devastation on Northern Italy and ended the independence of many of the city-states. On May 6, 1527, Spanish and German troops sacked Rome, ending the role of the papacy as the largest patron of Renaissance art and architecture. Yet even then, a new Renaissance called the Northern Renaissance began to develop, continuing the ideals of the great Italian Renaissance.